MUM'S WITCH

BASE FEAR: BOOK 4

S.C. FISHER

Copyright © 2023 by S.C. Fisher

Published by Raven Tale Publishing

All rights reserved.

This book may not be duplicated in any way without the express written consent of the publisher, except in the form of brief excerpts or quotations for the purposes of review.

The information contained herein is for the personal use of the reader and may not be incorporated in any commercial programs or other books, databases, or any kind of software without written consent of the publisher or author. Making copies of this book or any portion of it, for any purpose is a violation of United States copyright laws.

This is a work of fiction. Names, characters, places, and incidents either are the product of the author's imagination or are used fictitiously. Any resemblance to actual persons, living or dead, events, or locales is entirely coincidental.

ISBN: 9798389287501

✽ Created with Vellum

1

DAY 7 – 6:30 HRS

I woke Becca unreasonably early on Sunday morning, hopeful that the mug of coffee in my hands would serve as acceptable currency to make up for it. It didn't. My sister launched a pillow at my head that almost knocked the mug sideways. She wasn't much of a morning person.

"I know you're not creeping into my room at..." she paused to squint at the alarm clock on the nightstand, continuing in a growl, "six thirty on a Sunday! What is wrong with you, Olly? Not cool."

Saying nothing, I held out the coffee mug. Becca's scowl deepened as she sat up with the sheets bunched at her chest.

"I don't want coffee," she snapped, shaking her head. "I want to sleep! You know, that thing normal people do at the weekend?"

"Don't flatter yourself with normal," I retorted, and stepped aside when the second pillow came hurtling towards me. Maybe I deserved that one.

"You better have a good excuse."

She kicked back the comforter and I handed off the coffee,

waiting for her to take a long pull before I started to fill her in on the happenings from the night before: Jennifer, the berries, the showers. I even lifted my shirt to show off the scabbed over cut in my navel. She listened to me babble until her mug was drained, then she set it down in favour of jabbing a finger at my head.

"That explains why your hair looks like shit."

Self-conscious, I touched the ends of my curls, which were matted and fluffy through lack of recent care. I didn't need to examine the dresser mirror to know that I looked like I'd been buried then dug back up again.

"My hair isn't important," I defended, forcing myself to lower my hands.

"Then what is? Jennifer Reitner? She probably got sick and went home."

I growled, frustrated. Hadn't Becca been listening to a single word I said?

"She didn't. The witch got her, like she got Charlie and Tiff, and probably Mrs. Pedlow."

"Olly, listen to yourself, this is insane. You sound like Hayley!"

"Maybe Hayley isn't wrong. Agnes will come for us, too. I can't sit here and wait for it. I have to do something!"

Grimacing, Becca rubbed her forehead. I wondered if it was the early morning or my ranting that was giving her the headache she was trying to massage into submission.

"What is it that you want from me?"

I couldn't quite manage to head my smirk off at the pass. I knew she would cave. There was no way my sister would leave me to unravel the mystery on my own, especially when I called my own safety into question. With Becca, you had to know what buttons to push, then push them hard.

That was how we found ourselves on the bus to Bury St.

Edmunds at seven thirty on a frosty Sunday, Becca glowering as she cupped her travel mug, and me with a bobble hat shoved down over my ears to hide the monstrous state of my hair.

"For the record, I still think this is nuts." Becca flashed me the stink-eye. "I'm here to humour you and for the free burger you promised me."

I nodded and sank back into the seat, grimacing when the metal frame dug into my shoulders. The seat pad was so thin and pathetic that I could feel every individual bar and screw despite the layering of my sweater and jacket. Outside, the clouds started to spit fat raindrops diagonally onto the sidewalk. They splattered against the window, exploding on contact with the glass, and I looked away when I remembered how the spider-berries had met the same fate on the shower room tiles.

"You'll get your burger." I shifted to meet Becca's eyes. "And I'm not nuts. You'll see."

Becca sipped from her mug, eyes trained on me over the rim.

"We've all been through a lot. I get it. Sometimes, we look for reasons for..."

"That's not what this is."

"Isn't it?"

I pulled my gaze away, giving the empty bus a quick sweep. I wouldn't deny that I was on edge, constantly awaiting the next catastrophe, but I was adamant that I wasn't imagining anything. I nearly flinched when Becca's fingertips slid against my own. I'd been lost in thought, and hardly expected her comfort when she was so mad at me for dragging her out of her bed. However, when I looked down, her smaller, softer hand gripped mine. I smiled.

"It's not," I said, though less angry than I'd been moments ago. "I know it sounds ridiculous, I know it's not the kind of thing that either of us would usually believe, but I feel it, Becca. There's evil at Mildenhall."

"I can't think of a single person who'd want to hurt Charlie, Tiff, Mrs. Pedlow, or Jenny," she said, squeezing my fingers once then letting go. "I can't think of a single person at Mildenhall who'd want to hurt anyone."

I arranged my hands in my lap then rubbed them vigorously against each other to encourage warmth to spread through my bones. It didn't help. The weather outside and the broken bus heater worked against me in tandem. I wished I'd stopped to find my gloves before we'd left the house but there hadn't been time. Every second was crucial.

"I can." I peered into my sister's face, breathing harder, faster, more erratically. "The witch is real and she wants her seven souls. She already has four. We have to stop her before she gets the rest."

Becca let me be after that. She curled against the window - somehow immune to the cold that permeated the misted glass - and cradled her travel mug. I was fine with the distance. I needed time with my thoughts. Time to work out my next move.

The bus slowed to a stop a short walk from the old market square. We shuffled off the steps, limbs barely working in the extreme cold, and thanked the driver before the doors slid closed. The bus pulled away from the sidewalk and I started walking, past the rows of locked stores and darkened buildings. Sundays in England were weird; slow, dismal days, where the superstores closed early and the smaller businesses didn't bother opening at all. It was difficult to get used to the sedentary pace of life, coming from America, where there's something to see or do every hour of every day.

Becca caught up to me as I crossed the cobbled ground and slipped her arm through mine, suggesting that her pissy mood had passed. Our destination stuck out from the top corner of the square like a sore thumb: Moyse's Hall, where the county's largest collection of historical witchcraft related artefacts were catalogued and housed.

The building dated back to the medieval period, according to the information plaque set to the left of the studded door. My research had informed me that it'd served many purposes over the centuries, from police station to jail to poor house, before being repurposed as a museum for the last hundred years. I remembered taking a trip to the hall with school a few grades back, and how I'd wandered the exhibits with Tiff and Charlie giggling at my side. Then, I hadn't been much interested in what the place had to offer, but times changed and so did people. If there was a way to stop Agnes Tippet then I was hopeful I would find it here.

I covered the entrance fee for us both and listened with a polite smile as the attendant rattled off a list of the temporary exhibits the hall was hosting. Finally, she pushed a couple of information pamphlets into my hand and we were allowed to begin our tour. Becca trailed behind, letting me lead the way. I had no desire to stop and marvel at any of the other curiosities; the civil war gauntlets that winked at me from inside their cabinet; the greying lock of hair that belonged to a long-dead French queen; the oil painting of a handsome but too-young soldier in his World War II uniform. None of them called out to me or snared my attention. They couldn't possibly compete with the oddities I sought.

I knew where I was headed without glancing at the signs and so I ascended a set of stairs, lined with the works of local artists, with my sister on my heels. She didn't question where we were going. Her head turned as we passed by a room full of clocks, tick-tocking away with maddening incessancy, but she didn't pause. Our mission was far too important.

The case of mummified cats was the first thing I saw when I

entered the final room in the upper corridor. Becca stopped next to me, a gasp rising in her throat.

"Like Magic," she murmured.

But they weren't. These unfortunate felines had breathed their last breaths centuries ago. Their furless, exsanguinated bodies were far more pathetic by comparison. They had shrivelled like plums in the sun, their skin having shrunk so much that it appeared painted onto their bones. Each one was pinned to the back of the case to be displayed in all their brutal glory. Rigid, fragile, and repulsive. At least Magic had been granted the dignity of a shallow grave.

I approached the case to read the information cards, pulling out my cell to snap pictures of anything that might be useful. I rediscovered a lot of facts I'd already known and soon found myself hurrying from one display to another; from dead cats over to witch bottles then onto leather bound spell books that were closed to prying eyes. Probably for the best, all things considered. Who knew what kind of trouble could be summoned from within their unholy pages?

I was so caught up in it all that I hadn't noticed Becca slink off to the window that overlooked the square. Not until the man's voice called it to my attention.

"They used to execute the witches out there," he said, kind of jovially considering the subject matter. "Some historians believe that Matthew Hopkins was responsible for the deaths of over 300 accused individuals, but we simply don't have the written records to prove it."

He sauntered into the room, grinning, hands clasped behind his back, to interrupt my camera flash. I lowered the cell, hastily pushing it under my sleeve. I wondered if I'd contravened some kind of rule but the guy encouraged me to continue with a jerk of his head.

"Take as many pictures as you like. It's great to see people your age with an interest in history."

I returned his smile just long enough to allow me to evaluate the man, whose tweed jacket and museum nametag suggested he was harmless enough. He gazed back at me from behind a pair of round spectacles and a thick fringe of grey hair that flopped over the ridge of his forehead.

"They burned women? Out there?" Becca sounded justifiably horrified.

The guy – Patrick, according to the tag – wheeled round to my sister with the kind of enthusiasm that made me think he would be prepared to talk for as long as we were prepared to listen.

"No, they were hung. We didn't burn many witches in England," he said with a misplaced chuckle. "Not all of the accused were women, either. About ten percent of all witch trial victims were male."

Victims. The word pierced me like a bullet. Agnes Tippet had been a victim once. Just a naive girl who had been so worried about starving to death over a harsh winter that she had made an awful choice. Now, though, she was claiming victims of her own, apparently without remorse. I had to wonder how many of us had that kind of darkness lying dormant inside. Who among us could hurt others in order to save our own skin? *Soul, not skin*, I had to remind myself. Agnes was fighting for her soul, and that was a different ballgame. A soul undeniably upped the stakes and, maybe in her position, I would have done the exact same to avoid the fires of eternal damnation.

"Is there something specific you girls are looking for?" asked Patrick, his voice cleaving my thoughts.

I could feel Becca staring, waiting for guidance, but I didn't turn to acknowledge her. My focus was entirely on Patrick, whose smile hadn't wavered even when his brow expectantly arched.

"Actually, yeah, there is." I slid my cell out from my sleeve to wave it under the guy's nose. "You mind if I record you answering some questions? It's for a Halloween article in the school paper."

If he sensed my lie then he didn't challenge me. I dialled up the wattage on my smile to make it shine a little brighter, hoping it might sway his decision. Turned out it was an unnecessary manipulation because his whole face tensed with excitement at the prospect. Before I knew it, he had pulled out a few chairs from the staff room and arranged us in front of the case of cats to conduct our interview, like he expected to be appearing on the ten o'clock news.

"Fire away!" he prompted, once we had folded ourselves into the plastic seats.

I thrust my phone out then clicked the record button onscreen. Our voices echoed in the high-ceilinged room but not enough to affect the quality of the recording. It was a stroke of genius, I thought. Now, whatever wisdom Patrick had to impart would be documented, word for word, rather than butchered beyond recognition when I tried to relay it to Hayley and Rose.

"So... why did the witch trials start in England?"

I didn't really care. Some sort of explanation for it existed in the recesses of my mind, but it was useless information as far as the witch of Mum's Woods was concerned. Regardless, I had to make our request look genuine, and diving right into questions about Agnes Tippet would have looked suspicious.

"Ah, that's an interesting story," Patrick said, growing more animated.

Maybe it was, however, somewhere between King James I and a cursed fleet of ships, I started to get antsy. My desire to hear about Agnes - to know the details of her life and her death -

eclipsed my interest in anything else. Unfortunately, there was no way of saying as much to Patrick without exposing ourselves for the frauds we were, so I sat quietly, listening and working hard to maintain a look of moderate attentiveness. Becca was having less trouble with that than me. As Patrick launched into a speech about some book called *Daemonologie* that had been written by the crazy, witch-obsessed English king, she leaned further and further forward in her seat. She wasn't just hanging off the guy's every word, she was throwing grappling hooks at each syllable and abseiling down them. By the time he had answered to his own satisfaction, he was utterly breathless and gleeful. A sly glance at the clock told me we'd already wasted nearly an hour of our time. Frustrated by the realisation, I worded my next question far less tactfully.

"What can you tell us about local cases? Trials that happened around the Mildenhall area."

"Well, Matthew Hopkins came to Suffolk when..."

"No," I interjected, coolly, disregarding the surprise in Patrick's eyes. "We were hoping to feature a specific case. Since the article's coming out at Halloween, we wanted to include local myth. You know, scare the pants off the readers."

I shrugged, adding a laugh to sell it. Becca dutifully joined in.

"You're talking about the legend of Agnes Tippet, right?"

Our laughter faded but Patrick's smirk didn't. I barely managed to duck my head in confirmation. Although Becca didn't really believe me when it came down to it, she froze at the mention of the witch, too. From my peripheral vision, I watched her sweater cling to her tightened bicep, which strained as she gripped the base of her seat.

"Our teacher told us a little, and we've heard stuff from other kids, but we want the truth. From a professional."

Patrick pursed his lips and, for one horrible moment, I

wondered if he was going to deny the request. The guy probably had history degrees coming out the wazoo; maybe he considered answering questions about curses and monsters to be beneath him.

"We don't have any artefacts specifically relating to Agnes, but I could tell you what I know, I suppose. Anecdotally speaking, of course."

It was tough to maintain my calm facade when I replied, "That could work."

Becca was far less cool about it.

"Awesome! The other kids will love it. Anything you can think of is amazing!"

In the pause that followed, I realised from the way Patrick puffed out his chest and beamed that he was flattered, rather than freaked out by Becca's intensity. I poked my sister's hand to convey my approval. Patrick rolled up the sleeves of his stuffy-looking jacket and ploughed right into the tale as if he was narrating an episode of *The Twilight Zone*.

"There are certain details about Agnes Tippet's story that every Mildenhall native will know as well as the back of their own hand; her age, her situation, the nature of her unusual 'talent'. However, there are just as many details that have been lost to time, and the retelling of a tale that was – for a while - considered too awful and gruesome to relay to younger generations."

I checked my cell, paranoid that the recording might have switched itself off. The speaker symbol flashed on and relief warmed the pit of my stomach.

"The day that Agnes agreed to scry for Elizabeth Benjamin was the day she signed her own death warrant. What Agnes claimed to have seen would have been best kept secret but, with youth and innocence working against her, she spoke without consideration for the consequences."

"What did she say?"

I hissed at Becca whilst Patrick looked irked, and she soon got the message to zip her mouth. It was a shame that Agnes hadn't done the same.

"Elizabeth had three children and another on the way. When Agnes searched her future, she foresaw their deaths. According to Agnes, the Benjamin children would be taken by a fever, and she urged Elizabeth to be vigilant. Unfortunately for both women, Elizabeth wasn't that much of a believer. She laughed off Agnes' warning. Within the month, her children - including the babe in her womb- were dead."

I imagined that was enough to cure the woman's scepticism but I kept that thought to myself, cognisant of the spite in it.

"Elizabeth herself was in a bad way, likely suffering from the Smallpox that took her children, but she made sure to use the last of her strength to point the finger of blame squarely at Agnes. The Benjamins labelled Agnes a witch and, overcome with grief and rage, they gathered together a mob. As Elizabeth took her last breath, Agnes was dragged from her home and forced into the woods."

Outside in the market square a child screamed and the three of us startled. We exchanged glances, interspersed with nervous laughter.

"What happened then?" Becca asked.

Patrick took a deep breath.

"They cut branches from the sturdiest yew tree they could find, then they drove them through Agnes' elbows and knees to stake her to the ground. If the dead were ever to walk the earth again, like the book of *Revelations* suggests, they didn't want to risk a witch being among them. Plus, hanging could be a relatively quick death if you were lucky enough to break your neck. The Benjamins wanted Agnes to suffer, like Elizabeth and her children had."

"That's awful."

Patrick murmured his agreement. "Yes, it was, but vigilante justice wasn't unheard of back in those days. When Agnes' body was eventually discovered, the Benjamins readily confessed to the crime. Surviving court records show that they were acquitted. Agnes had made her 'gifts' known and that was a dangerous thing to do indeed."

I couldn't disagree there.

"What about the rest of the story?" Becca pressed. "Like her body being buried under the 'twisted tree'... the seven souls..."

Patrick guffawed and slapped his knee in a gesture I'd only ever seen executed before in the movies. His Irish lilt intensified with his amusement.

"Nobody can say for sure where she was eventually laid to rest. The only information we have states that her body was interred on 'unhallowed ground', as all suspected witches were. Not much to go on."

"And the poem? Agnes' ghost?" When Patrick's eyes fixed on me, curious and perhaps suspicious, I added in a rush, "It's a Halloween article. We want to include the creepiest parts of the story."

"I can't say that I personally believe in ghosts and monsters or what have you, but some are adamant that Agnes' restless spirit goes on in some form."

"How would someone wake her up, if they wanted to?"

Patrick grinned. "You thinking about it?"

"No," I said, and my voice echoed uncomfortably from the rafters.

"A blood sacrifice, I believe. Then, allegedly, Agnes will rise forth to claim the souls of seven, hoping to bargain her freedom with the devil in return. Whoever raises the witch might mark her victims for her using a handful of berries from the same tree she's buried beneath."

I wanted to puke. Or maybe pass out. I couldn't decide

which. Since neither was a viable option, I gawked at Patrick, totally dumb.

"How do we kill her?" I blurted out, no longer caring how unbalanced I sounded or looked. Patrick only blinked at me, eyes owlish from behind his lenses.

"She means, does the story say how to return the witch to the grave?" Becca jumped to my rescue. She flashed a winning smile at Patrick as she lied, "We want to be really thorough. Makes for a great read."

He no longer appeared convinced. Regardless, he must not have been able to resist finishing his tale.

"Nobody knows. You've heard the rhyme, passed down from parent to child, and so on; *'should Aggie set her sights on you, there is nothing God himself can do.'* Perhaps all that can be done is to let the witch have her way."

I don't recall turning off the recording; rising from my chair; shaking Patrick's hand; leaving the museum. I only know that I somehow found the ability to do all of those things because Becca told me so later on, when we sat at our restaurant table, letting our burgers go cold. Neither one of us had much of an appetite when all we could think of was poisoned berries and dead girls.

We listened to the recording once, twice, three times, as we sipped at our coke floats. By then, I could recite it word for word, and it was almost funny to me how I'd worried that I might not be able to remember everything Patrick had to say. I knew now that if I lived to be a hundred and change, I wouldn't forget a single word. The recording ended for a fourth time and I looked down at my full plate. The puddle of grease that had oozed out from the burger patty had saturated the bun and reduced it to a soggy mess. As I reached for my phone, tired of hearing Patrick's voice, Becca's hand shot out to grip my wrist. Eyes misty, she held onto me ferociously, as if I was an anchor.

On the inside, I felt more like a sheet of paper fluttering in the wind.

"Olly..." she whispered, a tear running down the plane of her cheek, "I believe you now."

With that, I was no longer so alone.

2

DAY 8 – 18:27 HRS

It was unheard of for my friends to visit me at work and not try to take advantage of me by pleading for larger portions or free whipped cream. A statistical impossibility, even. Yet, there they were, gathered around the counter on stools, not one of them making a move to as much as sniff in the direction of the ice cream. It was downright eerie.

I wiped down the hygiene screens on autopilot as Becca filled Rose and Hayley in on our findings from Moyse's Hall. Whilst Hayley listened, rapt and attentive, her eyes gleaming with vindication, Rose adopted a more relaxed stance: her folded arms rested on the counter and she sat with her chin leaning upon them. More than anything she looked bored, with a pinch of cynical thrown in.

"What do you guys think?"

Becca finished talking and I flung the cloth down to wait for their verdict.

"I think it's about time you guys started taking me seriously. I wish I hated to say *'I was right and you were wrong'*, but I don't."

I rolled my eyes at Hayley, who had been the *'ha, ha, I told you so'* kid from birth. Then, we were all looking at Rose, waiting on her acceptance.

"I think you've all gone barmy," she said, drawing away from the counter. "Just in case you didn't get that, I'll translate it into 'American' for you: the three of you have lost your collective shit."

Nobody moved. Not even Rose, who stared Becca down with disdain.

"Come on, Rose..." Hayley attempted, only to find herself cut off by the pointer finger shoved in front of her nose. The owner of said finger – Rose –vibrated with poorly controlled rage.

"No. You can all piss off and die. I don't want to be dragged into this. I don't want to play your stupid games anymore!"

"Who's playing games?"

"We're being totally serious."

The legs of Rose's stool screeched against the floor as she shoved it backwards to allow herself to hop down. I backed up a bit, unsure of her intent as she fumbled with her jacket, which had been resting on her lap. I was glad I did when the berries rolled out of the inner pocket, wheeling across the counter then bouncing like miniscule ping pong balls at my feet. I jumped out of the way, haunted by the memory of dozens of pairs of legs marauding across my flesh. Seeing my reaction, Becca came to my aid. She ducked around the side of the counter and dropped to her knees to scoop the berries up with both hands.

"Careful!" I warned. She ignored me in favour of dropping the berries into the sink, where she proceeded to smash each one with her fist before washing them away with the faucet.

"I found them after lunch." Rose's tone was flat. "I don't know which one of you did it but it's bloody cruel."

"Rose, we didn't do that. Right?"

Becca and I nodded along with Hayley, who reached out

with both hands to Rose, beseeching and suddenly so much softer than she had been for days. Slowly, I was coming to realise what this – these God-damn berries - meant, and I suspected that Hayley had, too. Rose had been marked for the witch.

"We wouldn't."

"I swear we had nothing to do with it."

As we rushed to offer our assurances, Rose backed off, shaking her head so hard that her bangs tumbled from her ponytail. Fire blazed in her eyes, and her chin quivered and dimpled. The tears started soon after, obviously without her consent. Rose balled her fists against them, and us.

"I don't want to hear it!" she yelled. A couple of heads poked out of neighbouring stores – vendors, curious as to what all the fuss was about. They didn't linger long, though, driven back behind their counters by Rose's fearsome scowl, which she aimed like a semi-automatic at anyone who breathed her way.

"Shut up! People are staring," hissed Hayley. She moved to grab Rose's sleeve and tug her back onto her stool. Rose avoided the snare effortlessly, sidestepping and pushing her arms behind her back so they were out of reach.

"Don't touch me. I'm done with you lot and your stupid stories. You can go to hell!"

We watched Rose storm out of the Exchange in varying degrees of shock and embarrassment. Her ponytail swished violently as she hurried along, desperate to be away from the three of us and our perceived lies. The only problem was, we weren't lying. Rose was in danger and, if she refused to listen, there would be no way we could help her.

"Should someone go after her or...?"

Becca left the question hanging. It went unanswered for the longest time whilst we exchanged puzzled looks and nibbled on fingernails, bottom lips, and anything in easy reach.

"No," Hayley decided. "Let her calm down. I'll text her later and see if I can talk sense into her."

I went back to tidying my already pristine workspace just to have something to do with my hands. Lately, the more idle they were, the more they trembled, and it was getting harder to hide. Once I'd finished disinfecting the scoops for the third time since the start of my shift, I fixed a couple of chocolate cones for Becca and Hayley. Mr. Maroney would ride my ass to Hell and back for giving away the stock, but I'd deal with it. He wasn't so scary in comparison to a three hundred year old dead chick with a taste for murder.

As Becca licked at the edges of her cone to catch the melting drips, Hayley watched me load the dishwasher. It took all of twenty seconds and then I was back to being inactive and anxious.

"I believe you guys. All along, I've thought there was more to Charlie's disappearance than the cops said. My sister didn't run away. She was taken."

My eyes flickered closed for a second as memories of everything that was inherently 'Charlie' rushed me: the sound of her laughter, the way she'd dance to commercial music whilst singing along with the jingles, how she claimed to enjoy the rum and raisin flavour we stocked every Spring, even though we all knew it was old person ice cream.

"What do we do?" Becca asked, between downhearted licks.

"We can't let Agnes take Rose."

It was odd to find myself as Rose Anderson's advocate, considering that we had a complex history. Regardless of her snippy attitude and occasionally poisonous tongue, she didn't deserve to be left to Agnes' mercy - which was in short supply to begin with.

"We won't. Now we know who and what we're dealing with, we can work out a plan. We can get rid of her."

Patrick had seemed uncertain of that, as was I. If neither the legend nor the rhyme detailed how to banish the witch, was it possible? My pessimistic nature had me leaning hard into 'no'. Maybe all that could be done was to wait for the witch to take her seven souls, and pray that you wouldn't be one of them. It was a depressing idea, but we were living in depressing times.

"Who's controlling her?"

Taken aback, we both looked at Becca. She finished the remnants of her cone by jamming the second half into her mouth whole, and crunching with passion. Chocolate stained her lips and the surrounding skin, so I handed her a stack of napkins to address the mess.

"Someone has to be controlling the witch. Somebody had to raise her. Now, they're picking out her victims by planting the berries on them," she continued, after she had scrubbed away the worst of it. "Patrick said so."

She was right. The museum guide had outlined it for us, however, my thoughts had been too clouded by the endless possibilities of what had become of Charlie and Tiff. Now, there was no way to avoid it; a sickening, terrible realisation. Someone in Mildenhall wanted me and my friends gone. Permanently. Somebody was as much of a killer as Agnes. I hadn't the first clue as to who it could be. We didn't mix with the popular crowd but we weren't so low down on the social totem pole that our bellies were scraping the dirt, either. As far as I knew, nobody despised any of us, which meant nothing in the grand scheme of things. Maybe Hayley had turned down the wrong guy, angling for a date: maybe Tiff had piqued some girl's jealousy with her quirky style and effortless grace: maybe I'd passed one too many notes in History and driven Mr. Maroney over the edge. There was no possible way to tell what crime had been committed, or which one of us had perpetrated it.

"We need a list of suspects. Also a way to keep the witch

away from us. Let's start there," Hayley suggested. "Prioritise. If anything happens to us then we can't stop Agnes, or find my sister and Tiff."

Poor Jenny, I mused, *so low down on our list that she doesn't score a mention.* Nevertheless, she was in an arguably better position than Mrs. Pedlow, who was beyond the realms of saving, lying mottled and prone somewhere on a coroner's slab. Without bodies, we couldn't be entirely sure that the three missing girls were dead. Whilst there was barely enough hope left inside to buoy me, I clung to those slivers with both hands and an iron grip.

"We saw witch bottles at the museum. The card said people used those to protect themselves from magic. We could start there?"

Wisely, Becca skirted around the topic of the mummified cats laid out in their glass coffins. There was no way Hayley would want to hear about those when Magic's loss was so fresh. Perhaps, though, I was beginning to understand Charlie's willingness to sacrifice the beloved family pet when the alternative had been Agnes.

"I bet Charlie has some books I can work from. I'll make one for Rose, too."

With Hayley volunteering her efforts with the witch bottles, that left me and Becca on research duty. I was happy to do it since we'd proved an effective team so far. Between the two of us, there was a much better chance that we would find a way to stop Agnes - if one existed in the first place.

"Okay, you do your thing, we'll do ours, and we can reconvene tomorrow after school."

"Should we maybe tell somebody? Our parents or the cops?"

It had felt like a dumb suggestion when it had unfurled in my head, but voicing it made me realise exactly how absurd it was. Like anyone would believe us about the witch. It had taken long enough for me to believe what I'd seen with my own two eyes.

"And make them think we're all..." Hayley tailed off. She completed her sentence by winding her pointer finger in the air next to her head. The universally recognised sign for 'cracked'.

"They'd have to listen to three of us," I insisted. Apparently, I was prepared to die on this hill. "It's not like crazy things haven't been happening around here."

"She's right. Can you really see Dad believing that our friends are being kidnapped by some bitch who croaked hundreds of years ago?"

"Or that Mrs. Pedlow was murdered?" Hayley added, dropping her voice to a whisper. We'd already attracted enough attention for one evening.

Thinking about our old piano teacher, my fingers drifted unconsciously to the natural dip at the base of my neck. Nearby, a kid popped their gum and I jumped, my hand falling away. They were right. I might have been reluctant to admit it, but they were. Our parents were logical, intelligent, responsible people. Nobody with even one of those qualities would swallow the idea of an urban legend come to life. It was way too Hollywood.

Our next move had been decided, and so Hayley left the parlour after hugging us both tightly and making us swear to stick together at all times. There were no arguments. I didn't think I'd risk peeing alone with everything going on around us.

As I had predicted, the most action I saw for the rest of the evening was when a woman accidentally dropped her soda by the fountain and I volunteered to help her mop the spill. Becca waited for me at the counter, then we played tic-tac-toe on the ordering pad whilst we ate through a tub of jellybeans that were past their best before date. We didn't talk about Agnes, if only to forget for a few hours.

Though it seemed like the hands on the clock had started to

tick backwards, the end of my shift eventually arrived, and I was able to pull the shutters down in front of the store. The walk home turned into a jog when some dog in a yard howled and I almost dropped dead on the spot. I hadn't thought of myself as a coward before but the shoe seemed to fit and I was lacing it up.

At home, my sister and I picked at the plates of cold steak and salad that Mom had left covered in the refrigerator. Taped to the door was a note that told us our parents were at one of Dad's work functions and that we shouldn't expect them back before we were asleep, which was parent code for *'your asses are toast if you're not in bed when we get home'*. Usually, I wouldn't have minded. That night, I watched the doors, the windows, and the clock alternately, expecting the worst from them all.

My stomach had quit rumbling for real food days ago – assuming that ice cream didn't constitute as a meal - and I was aware from the way my jeans hung lower on my hips that I was unintentionally losing weight. Still, I couldn't manage to force myself into eating close to half of what Mom had arranged on the plate. I guiltily scraped too much food into the garbage, then went upstairs to get ready for bed. We changed in my bedroom, backs turned to allow some small degree of privacy. We used the bathroom together too, and I'm not ashamed to admit that I did not, in fact, pee alone that night. When your life is hanging in the balance, things like privacy tend to become trivial. If it hadn't done so already, it definitely took a backseat when Becca and I finished by crawling under her quilt to tangle up in each other. It didn't feel safe to be separated.

As we lay on our backs in the darkness, our gentle breaths synchronised thanks to the proximity of our bodies. More time than I could quantify passed. I remained stiff and uncomfortable, my tense body at odds with the way it sank into Becca's marshmallow mattress. Regardless of how I tried, I couldn't switch my brain off; couldn't halt the constant churn of newly acquired information and rampant speculation that flooded the synapses.

"Olly?"

I guess, neither could Becca.

"Yeah?" I turned my head, bringing us nose to nose.

"Do you think we can beat it?"

She spoke like the *'it'* in question was a cancer. In a way, I supposed it was. Something dark, parasitic, and sinister had hooked its claws into us. Given the chance, it would consume us, cell by cell, if we failed to find the means to cut it out or burn it away first.

"Yes. I know we can," I lied.

Becca snuggled closer with a sigh. She draped her arm across my midsection then latched her fingers onto the curve of my hip until we were slotted together with knees and elbows at perfect angles to each other. I didn't utter a complaint when her icy feet made contact with my bare ankles. I was too busy re-examining her question, and the deception I'd managed to counter it with without flinching.

Do you think we can beat it? Yes.

There wasn't room for another consideration. I didn't want to die and I couldn't tolerate losing my sister. There were so many things we had left to do, countless firsts to experience, and so much of the world and ourselves to explore. We were supposed to go on vacations together - get matching tattoos - watch each other graduate - interrogate future boyfriends until they cried out of honest-to-God fear. We were supposed to be swaddled in the magical invincibility cloak of youth for many years to come. We were supposed to *live*. Time should have been on our side. It wasn't fair to think that maybe it suddenly wasn't.

Do you think we can beat it? An echo, mocking me. *I know we can.*

Was it strictly a lie if you wanted it to be true bad enough?

Yes. Yes, it was.

3

DAY 9 – 19:00 HRS

I found out from Becca on the bus ride home from school that Rose had been a no-show. It wasn't like her to be absent without cause. Her parents were both third generation military and really big on accountability. Unless she was doubled over the toilet, puking or pooping out an internal organ, there was no justifiable reason to miss class, in their book. Maybe that was why Rose could be such a bitch sometimes: there was so much expected of her that the fear of disappointing her folks had her constantly lashing out.

Becca told me the news in a shaky voice. We both knew what it could mean. A few rows ahead, Hayley turned in her seat to make frequent eye contact with us. I could tell from her pallid complexion that she too was thinking the worst.

After the bus dropped us outside the camp gates, we huddled together on the sidewalk, waiting for the rest of the students to scatter as the rain came down in sheets. We decided on heading back to my house since the tension was thick in the air at Hayley's. The lack of new leads on Charlie was gnawing away at their parents like some flesh-eating superbug. According to Hayley, Mrs. Hill barely crawled out from her bed at all whilst

Mr. Hill spent hours locked away in the home office with the curtains drawn and a bottle of something top shelf for company.

When the three of us bundled through the front door – half drowned and shivering – our mom took one sour look at us as we dripped rainwater onto the beige carpet. She clicked her tongue in discontent but pressed towels warm from the dryer directly into our hands, anyway. Then, she fixed us hot chocolate with cinnamon and a plate stacked with sandwiches, as we changed into dry socks and wrung the moisture from our hair. Once she'd fussed over us to her satisfaction, Mom dismissed us with the leftovers and very explicit instructions not to bother her whilst she finished drafting the rota for the store. The words *'on pain of death'* were expressly spoken, not implied, and we acquiesced without doubting how serious she was. It would be better to be upstairs in my room, out of earshot, anyhow. We had things to discuss; things that I was confident we didn't want a parent to overhear.

"Rose didn't answer any of the messages I sent her last night or this morning. I couldn't find anything useful in Charlie's books about how to make witch bottles, either."

Rain lashed against the windowpane, drawing shivers from the three of us, who recalled the discomfort of being soaked through by it hours ago. The sound was overshadowed by the wind howling around the outside walls. I had never been afraid of weather before, however, I had never been hunted by a monster before. Therefore, the subtle tip-tap of a tree branch on the frame was nearly enough to unspool me.

Hayley picked at the crust of the PB and J in her hand, flaking it off with her fingernail. Purple polish shimmered as the light hit it just so, and I looked down at my own bitten-to-the-quick nails.

"I tried calling Rose. It went right through to voicemail."

I stuffed the rest of my sandwich into my mouth. Chewing

was a struggle since my saliva glands were running dry. I managed to force down the crust, even with peanut butter sticking to the roof of my mouth, entrapping my tongue. I'd never enjoyed food less than I had in the past week, and that included the time I'd had my tonsils removed and my throat was so raw that swallowing was akin to being punched in the neck.

"Call again," Hayley encouraged, and my sister gamely shuffled her cell out of her pocket.

With the call on speaker, we could all listen to the persistent ring that would surely go answered. On and on it went, alongside the drumming of the rain, and Hayley grew visibly more distressed as each peel receded into the next.

"We should never have let her go," she said. Becca didn't look up from disconnecting the call, which had finally been picked up by voicemail.

"We couldn't have stopped her. You know what Rose is like when she's made up her mind."

"She wasn't thinking straight," I agreed. "We did what we could."

Hayley was dubious. She raked a hand through her hair, mussing it so that the shorter layers stood on end, the way they do when you rub a balloon over your head and static electricity works its will.

"I should go over there. Rose's parents are away with work. Nobody will know if... if anything bad has happened."

It was the most sensible option remaining. However, there was no way I was prepared to let Hayley venture to Rose's house when the witch was gunning for her. If Rose was sick - and making good on her threat to ignore us - then Agnes might show up at any moment. I had no clue what would happen to someone who stood in her way, and I didn't want Hayley to find out.

"We'll come with you."

"Right. Nobody goes anywhere alone from now on."

I'd known I could count on Becca's agreement. She was the best sister and friend anyone could have. There was nothing she wouldn't do for the people she cared about, whether on a regular day or in a pinch. Our parents claimed it was a declining quality – Dad with a hint of pride, Mom with a touch of concern. I guess she thought it was inevitable that my sweet sister's kindness would turn her into the world's doormat, but I knew Becca was capable of drawing lines when she needed. It smarted to admit that she was better than me in many ways. If Bec had been Charlie's best friend, she never would have missed the widening chasm between them in the first place.

"You guys don't have to do that." Hayley reassured us with a smile that highlighted the bags under her eyes. None of us had been sleeping much and the effects of fatigue were more obvious on some than others.

The angle of the rain changed abruptly, the rhythm and pitch of the pattering altering along with it. Water pounded straight down on the roof, rather than slanting against the window. We ignored it, as well as the tree branch clipping the outer sill.

"We do. We're here for you."

"Don't be dumb."

I was less diplomatic than Becca, having inherited the lion's share of Mom's no-bullshit approach to life. That didn't mean that what I had to say was any less valid just because it was less fluffy. Of course it would be the actual definition of stupid to run off alone when a supernatural entity was marking us for death. Often, the advice a person needs to hear most is not the advice they're seeking. Hayley seemed to understand, and she didn't react badly to my bluntness.

"Okay, we'll go together. Do you want to wait for the rain to..."

She didn't finish. There wasn't time.

The rapping at the window escalated from persistent to unremitting, no longer something we could attribute to weather alone. Our heads swivelled to the sound and Becca warily moved towards it whilst Hayley shrank back. I stayed where I was, fixed to the spot, my brain working sluggishly. If I had been thinking, I'd have grabbed hold of my sister and dived right out of harm's way. Seconds later, we paid for our indecision.

Shattering. Glass showering the carpet. Becca screaming.

The tree limb shot through the gaping hole it had punched in the glass, coiling into the air as it rose snake-like in front of Becca's face. The entire tree suddenly leaned against the side of the house, its naked branches unfurling and twisting into my bedroom, as though they were living entities.

It was impossible.

A building cry choked me and I jerked into action. Becca remained rooted, watching the branches weave in and out of each other, creating rigid braids that defied plausibility. *Move,* my mind raged, *why won't you all move?*

"Look," Hayley whispered. Against every instinct that warned me not to, I did. From where I stood, I peered through the fragmented window and right into the fierce eyes of Agnes Tippett.

Her face was etched into the trunk that sagged against the frame, the branches hovering over Becca serving as her limbs in the absence of real appendages. Whilst I could pick out a slightly hooked nose set above thin lips, and the faint dimpling of a chin, that was as far as Agnes resembled a human girl. Her skin had adopted the hue and texture of the bark her features were moulded into, and the teeth visible behind the swell of her lip were a jagged row of canines that hinted at the promise of brutality. When her mouth stretched wider in order to unleash a shriek that could be described as prehistoric, we clapped our hands over our ears. Opportunistic, the wind barrelled into the room behind the rain, which soaked the carpet beneath my window. Agnes – the monster – strained against her corporal prison, teeth gnashing.

Sheets of composition flew off my music stand to whip around us then batter me in the side of the head as they scattered. The fleece blanket on the end of my bed curled upwards and struck Hayley. It wrapped around her upper body so that she was forced to fight against it with clawed hands. Her squeals added to the commotion and - blind but not deaf to the chaos unfolding – Mom showed up in the corridor to hammer on my door.

"What's going on in there? Girls? What the hell?" Her fists drove into the wood again and again. She rammed the door with her shoulder, though it refused to budge. "Let me in! Girls?! Let me in, damn it!"

I looked away for only a moment, distracted by the pounding as Mom attempted to gain entry.

"Mom!" I called, pleading. My heart started to sing as the door gave an inch under her weight. Her victory lasted a fraction of a second, then the door was slamming shut once more, the knob rattling as the gale twisted it the wrong way. I attempted to grab for it, trying to help Mom, and that presented Agnes with the opportunity she had needed.

The next howl that ripped from the witch flowed directly into the one that emerged from my sister. Becca's body slammed against the dresser. She found herself pinned there by the branch that had speared her right hand and driven straight through the wall behind. Impaled, she stretched on tiptoes with her arm above her head and blood coursing from the wound in her palm. Becca whimpered - tears and snot mingling on her upper lip - but she did not scream out again. Shock paled her, sucking the colour from her cheeks as fast as the blood poured from her hand.

"Becca!" I hollered her name at the same moment that Hayley dove for the extended branch with a booming bellow.

My hands seized my sister's shoulders and Hayley grabbed for Agnes' questing limb. I prepared to take the brunt of Becca's weight whilst Hayley wrenched the branch, snarling. She tugged, harder and harder, her grip like iron and her determination as strong. The beginnings of a cracking sound snaked through the gaps in the anarchy. The branch popped free with a squelch seconds before Hayley managed to snap it in half. Wounded, Agnes keened, and the tree-monster shrank away from the window to rock back to its regular spot in the yard. As though it had never moved to begin with. The rest of the tendrils whistled by, some scraping our cheeks bloody, but Hayley held her ground and waved the severed branch aloft like a warning.

I caught Becca in my arms as the door buckled to reveal Mom, panting and agitated, on the threshold. She surveyed the bedroom and the disarray with her mouth hanging. I was far too focussed on shrugging off my sweater to bind Becca's wound to bother stammering an explanation.

"What..."

Becca's breathing was noisy and concerning, her eyes glassy. I wrapped my arms around her to transfer some warmth to her body. She shuddered against me yet sweat beaded on her brow.

"Hos-hospital," I stuttered, beseeching. "She needs a hospital!"

Fortunately, Mom was several steps ahead of me, already fishing her car keys from her pocket as she crossed the room to transfer Becca from my arms to her own. I helped my sister stand straight, keeping the makeshift bandage tight to stem the bleeding.

"You'll be okay, honey."

Becca visibly calmed. The heaving of her chest receded and she focussed on Mom with a resurgence of clarity. Mom swept a lock of hair away from Becca's forehead, her chin quivering in her only display of emotion, before she locked it all down. An alarming amount of blood soaked through my sweater to seep onto Mom's, but she didn't appear to realise. Her stare icy, Mom regarded first me then Hayley, who tossed down the tree branch she wielded like it might have been alive.

"The storm... the tree broke the window... Becca was too close and... her hand..."

With narrowed eyes, Mom shook her head, and I bit my tongue to force it to be still. She could always tell when I was lying.

"I'll talk to you when I get back."

I nodded, not even the tiniest spark of resistance flaring inside me.

"Get this mess cleaned up, both of you, then, Hayley, you get yourself home. I'll be texting your mom in an hour to make sure."

"She probably won't answer," Hayley muttered, shifting debris around with the toe of her shoe. Too weary to argue, Mom chose to ignore the insolence. Glass and paper crunched beneath her heels as she strode out of the room - Becca in her charge - leaving me and Hayley to deal with the carnage. We stood for a time, surveying the scene without speaking. The rain continued to assault the roof, though the wind had died down considerably, and the storm no longer seemed as fearsome. Eventually, we had to move, which we did when the noise of Mom's car peeling away from the curb jolted us.

Hayley approached the window and pulled the curtains back completely, shaking pieces of glass and wood free. I stooped to collect sheet music on my way to join her and tried to ignore the way the paper fluttered in my badly trembling hands.

"Tomorrow, as soon as we can, we go see Rose," Hayley said. "We need to know she's okay."

"We can ditch class, if we have to."

"This is way more important than school. This is some *'final girl'* shit."

I drew up beside her at the window. We scanned the front yard together, leaning against each other for reassurance. The moon had all but disappeared behind the swollen clouds that had produced the earlier storm, but the light from the streetlamps provided enough visibility for our needs.

"Becca will be okay," Hayley promised, catching my eye. "Whoever controls the witch hasn't marked her. Agnes must have been trying to scare us off. Maybe she wants to keep us from helping Rose."

It made sense. The witch was closer to achieving her goal than I supposed she ever had been before, and there was no way she would want a bunch of kids ruining that for her. When I'd gotten close to Jennifer at the school, right before she was taken, Agnes had acted by unleashing the spider-berries on me. This stunt was another scare tactic – an attempt to dissuade us from trying to fight back. Agnes was playing dirty.

Hayley helped me to clear the worst of the crap, then disappeared home before my mom was scheduled to call hers. Mom never made idle threats, emergency room or not, and keeping on the better sides of our parents was vital if we wanted to retain our freedom. There was no way we could investigate Agnes Tippet if we were grounded until Christmas.

I scrubbed Becca's blood off my wall with hot water, a splash of bleach, and Dad's boot brush. I struggled with waves of nausea whilst I did so, especially when I noticed tattered skin on the surface of my dresser, and how the bubbles in the water grew to be tinged pink. By the time I'd finished, Dad had called to say he was joining Becca and Mom at the hospital, and I was forced to find something to cover over the hole in my window by myself. In the end, I decided on a piece of cardboard, fixed with military grade tape. Not exactly sturdy, or durable, or capable of holding a witch at bay, but the only materials available to me on short notice.

Whilst I boarded the window, I took one last look into the front yard. My eyes sought out the monstrous tree before I was aware of it. In the end, I chose to examine it - long and hard - rather than flinch away. I was relieved by but sceptical of what I saw; no face; no flailing branches; no Agnes. Just a tree.

I taped the defences in place and moved away to sit on the corner of my bed. The house was far too quiet without Becca or my parents, and I wasn't accustomed to such complete solitude. I had started to wish we had a pet when I remembered Magic – the tragedy of his ending – and brusquely changed my mind.

Dad had promised, via text, that he'd call the housing company in the morning and have the storm damage fixed. I doubted that would make any difference to how unexpectedly insecure I felt in my own home. In the end, it wouldn't matter. Cardboard or glass, Agnes was determined, and she was coming.

4

DAY 10 – 06:12 HRS

I hadn't wanted to sleep that night. Sleep would make me vulnerable.

After Hayley had left and I'd cleaned my room, I'd found myself on the couch, flipping through the music channels. My eyelids must have started to droop around midnight because all I could recall was a parade of bootcut jeans, neon crop tops, and a synth-electric guitar combo that I cranked up loud enough to rattle the remaining windows. I didn't succeed in staving off my exhaustion.

I blinked awake at barely past six, surprised by the blanket draped over me and the glass of water set out within reach on the coffee table. My cell, which I was pretty sure I'd fallen asleep clutching, lay beside the tumbler on its charging dock. It was such a 'Mom' thing to do that I knew immediately she must have come home. The clink of dishes coming from the kitchen was equally promising so I kicked free of the blanket to investigate.

She was fixing a pot of coffee when I rounded the doorway. Mom turned, detecting the slide of socks on linoleum, and bestowed me with a smile that didn't hold up against the threat of a yawn.

"What time did you get back?"

"About an hour ago. You were dead to the world so I thought it was best to leave you be."

"Becca?" I demanded, leaning in to return the hug Mom offered me. When I breathed her in, her typical scents of cucumber moisturiser and perfume had been overridden by antiseptic. I pulled back, sickened.

"No broken bones. They cleaned the wound and stitched her up, but it's likely there'll be permanent damage to the tendons and ligaments."

"Is she still at the hospital? Where's Dad?"

The expression of relief she had worn whilst explaining Becca's condition to me resettled into one of disgruntlement.

"She refused to stay. Nearly clawed a nurse's eyes out when she tried to put a hospital bracelet on her. I don't know what's gotten into that girl."

I stayed quiet and swallowed down the impulse to defend Becca's seemingly unreasonable actions. I knew exactly why she hadn't wanted to stay. We had already determined that we were safer against Aggie if we stuck together.

"Dad?" I probed.

She huffed and reached for the freshly brewed coffee. When she poured it into the mug at her fingertips, I noted it was a couple of shades darker than she usually preferred. She didn't bother adding creamer, either.

"Grabbing a few hours of shut eye before work. Lucky me, I get to open up today so this is the first of many," she said, shaking her mug at me. "Wish it was something stronger."

She finished the whole cup in less than a minute, her throat working tirelessly to swallow down the gulps.

"I have to shower. I stink. Bathroom's yours when I'm done. Don't wake Becca!"

I paused, unhappy with the instruction but also aware that

Mom was so close to the edge, it wasn't wise to start prodding her further towards it.

"I thought... I could stay here with Becca today," I said. "Since you and Dad have to go to work. I can take care of her."

The mug had barely touched the counter before Mom was refilling it again, stifling another yawn by pressing her mouth into her shoulder. I waited for her decision, toying with my fingers and rocking on the balls of my feet. She slurped her coffee, eyeing me over the rim.

"You've missed so much school lately," she hummed.

Hope surged in my heart. It wasn't an outright 'no'. I could work with that.

"I know, but I'm making up all of the work."

Lie. I hadn't asked anyone to borrow their notes from the classes I'd missed.

"I'd really like to make sure Becca is okay."

Not a lie. My sister's welfare was all I was thinking about.

"I have a couple of projects I can look over."

Definitely false. I hadn't been writing down my homework assignments since Charlie. Mom looked me up and down, evaluating, trying to determine if it was sincerity or something else that I exuded.

Inspiration struck and, in a last ditch effort, I added, "I can tidy the house and make dinner, too."

The deal was clinched, I could tell by the glimmer of relief in Mom's eyes. She nodded at me and topped up her mug, though she'd barely touched it in the first place.

"Okay, you can stay home, but let your sister rest, and don't take advantage of my good nature by playing me for a fool, Olivia."

"No, ma'am." I darted forwards to plant a kiss on my mother's cheek. "I swear, tonight, you'll be able to eat the delicious dinner I cook for you off of this very kitchen floor."

With a snort of amusement, Mom reached out to tuck my hair behind my ear.

"I'll stick to a plate, thanks."

As I reached for a mug from the drawer, Mom nudged the creamer towards me, then watched me as I fixed my drink. Just as I was starting to grow unnerved, she spoke - dropping her bomb and detonating it, too.

"I feel like you girls are hiding things from me. You'd tell me if there was something going on, wouldn't you?"

Startled, I almost dropped the teaspoon I was using to tip sugar into my coffee. Granules skittered across the counter and under the microwave, to add to my chore list. Mom didn't comment - didn't even frown - far too focussed on watching my face for signs that I was hiding something. Of course, I was, so I did my best to smile through the guilt that made my knees knock and my heart hammer.

"Nope, there's nothing, Mom. We're worried about our friends."

I stirred and tried not to flinch each time the spoon clipped the porcelain. Mom's sympathetic gaze was a burden that I struggled under, alongside the weight of keeping the truth hidden. It made me feel worse when she reached out to grasp my hand - the one that wasn't gripping the mug hard enough to fracture it into a million pieces.

"I know there's a lot going on right now; Mrs. Pedlow, Charlie, Tiff, and now that girl from school."

"Jennifer," I supplied. My stomach dipped. Another potential runaway, according to the cops. They thought it was an epidemic.

"It's so sad, all these young girls turning their backs on their families when they need their support most." She paused and I prayed to God that she was done. She continued. "You both know that you can talk to me and Dad about anything, right?"

"Yes, Mom."

My voice had faded to a whisper but I knew Mom had heard me from the way her lips sloped into a scowl. She obviously wasn't convinced and I could hardly blame her since I wasn't putting on much of a show. *Get a grip*, I chided myself.

"Are you sure, because..."

I cut Mom off, lunging towards her to grab her up in a hug that surprised the both of us. Nevertheless, she tucked me into her body and drew her arms around me.

"I'm sure, Mom. I promise that we're going to be okay."

I couldn't seem to stop lying. They were pouring from me like water from a spout, and I was fearful I'd soon start to drown in them. My mom, and my dad, deserved the truth from us but, when the truth was too strange and too terrible, what else could I do but offer them a version of it that was easier to digest?

First Mom left for work, then Dad a couple of hours later. Becca slept and I kept watch over her. Like I'd promised, I tidied and cleaned the house practically from top to bottom, mostly to keep my frenzied mind occupied. A few times, between chores and peeking into Becca's room, I tried to call Rose. In the end, I was sick of the sound of her voicemail greeting, which was way too chipper under the circumstances. Each time I rang, I left a message, but those went unanswered, too.

At lunchtime, Hayley called to let me know she wasn't in school either, and had been coerced into attending a family counselling session with her parents. She didn't exactly appear thrilled about it, however, she was grateful that her parents were taking baby steps towards healing. I bit my lip as she talked, not quite ready to give up on the idea that Charlie might still walk back through the door; or - at the very least - that we might be able to retrieve her from the witch's clutches. Tiff and Rose, too. It was stupid and it was more naïve than I liked to admit I was, so I said nothing and breathed through the sadness until it receded.

We decided to meet that evening to visit Rose. No going rogue and no hero shit. Aggie was a threat best faced as a united front, although preferably not at all. As we were well past the point of no return on that one, we swore we would wait for each other. Anything else wasn't worth the risk.

The next time I looked in on Becca, a little after two, I discovered her bed empty with the sheets strewn across the floor. Uneasy, I stumbled out of her room and towards the stairs. My mind raced in sync with my pulse, painting vivid pictures for me of all the worst fates that could have been measured upon my baby sister. Too panicked to call her name, I made for the stairs as best I could, though it was so difficult to move my legs that it felt like I was wading through caramel. I was nearly halfway downstairs when I realised that the bathroom light was flickering weakly – on, off, on, off, on – in a staccato rhythm that made me think of Morse code.

"Becca!" I spun myself round and scrambled back. The hall stretched endlessly before me as I dashed for the bathroom with my sister's name a chant on my lips.

There was a soft chinking noise as the bulb worked itself overtime. When I entered the bathroom, I half expected to find Becca playing with the cord, trying to prank me. I did indeed find my sister, though nothing about her appearance was remotely as I'd expected.

"Becca?" I touched her shoulder with one hand. She didn't react to my presence or look away from the mirror.

Dazed, she swayed from left to right, and my fingers gripped her flesh in response. Her injured hand hung useless at her side, awkward and bulky thanks to the layers upon layers of bandaging. She hadn't even changed out of her pyjamas.

"Becca, are you okay?" I tried again. She didn't blink, didn't acknowledge me at all beyond shucking my hand from her body with a violent shrug that may or may not have been intentional.

Finally, she stirred. With a hiss, she demanded, "What is that?"

Above us, the light continued pulsing and clicking, despite the fact that nobody worked the pull cord.

"What's what?" I spoke loudly and clearly, with my mouth positioned so close to Becca's face that she must have been able to feel the gust of my breath against her jaw. She didn't tic.

"I don't like it. Make it go away," she whined.

"Make what go away?" I repeated, frustrated.

Shaking her head, Becca dissolved into sobs that covered the sound of the overworked light bulb clicking and popping. *Why wouldn't it quit?* I shot a dirty look at the cord, which swayed mildly to mock me.

"I'm calling Mom."

The threat did nothing to move my sister, who could only find the strength to gaze at her own reflection. She cried harder than I'd known her to cry before and, truthfully, that unnerved me more than any visions of Agnes' making could.

"Becca!" I implored, but she leaned closer to the surface of the mirror and choked on more of her tears.

"Why... why won't... it... g-go?"

There was nothing I could do except watch my sister breakdown - too oblivious to the catalyst to fix anything. It must have been whatever drugs they had her on. She was simply whacked out, confused, and having some kind of reaction to the trauma her body had endured. Unfortunately, I had no idea how to bring her out of it, and the possibility of some kind of adverse reaction to her medicine heightened my anxiety. I was no doctor. What if she had a seizure? Stopped breathing? The possibilities were innumerable and horrendous.

Right as I was debating summoning Mom home from work,

Becca quietened. I looked from the cell in my hand to my sister, not quite believing it could be that simple. I was starting to hate being right.

"Go away!"

Becca let out a fierce scream as she pounded her wounded hand against the centre of the mirror, over and over.

"Stop!"

I barked the command at her and somehow she didn't hear it, or else she chose to ignore it. Her mummified fist drove into the glass and, whilst she whimpered around the fresh pain it brought her, she didn't stop. I worried for her stitches, which were hours old. Becca didn't: she whipped her arm back and forward so fast that she was blur of bandages and aggression.

"I have to make it go away."

Her arm dropped as she stepped back with tears leaking from both eyes. Before I could react, Becca had raised her other hand to her face and buried her nails into the soft flesh. With breathtaking savagery, she clawed from the top of her cheek to the corner of her lips. She howled as blood beaded from the wounds she'd drawn in her own skin, and so did I. It seemed to snap her out of her trance. Becca started to hyperventilate as soon as she realised what she had done, reeling away from the mirror with her hands flapping. Her fingers covered the bloody tracks but I pulled them away to slap a wash cloth in their place. The bleeding wasn't severe yet it turned my stomach, probably more from shock than anything. I hadn't expected whatever this was.

"What were you doing? What were you thinking?"

I was in her ruined face, shouting at her and spitting saliva, despite her surging tears. She tried to pull away. My hand remained in place, firm against the wash cloth that staunched the flow. Wild-eyed, she gawked at me, her head shaking from side to side.

"There was something on my face. A spot... it was like... like a berry," she insisted. "It wouldn't wash off."

For the first time, I realised that the cloth sandwiched between us was damp, dripping water onto my socks.

"I had to get it off. I *had* to."

Stiffening, I allowed Becca to take over the cloth pressed to her cheek. I almost fell against the counter, managing to grab onto the edge at the last possible moment. My legs, like Jell-O, quivered enough that I doubted their abilities.

"There was nothing there. I swear to you... there was nothing."

We sank down to the bathroom floor together. Our arms sought each other out like they were separate entities from our bodies, and the wash cloth fell from Becca's face in the process to reveal the damage. Not as bad as I'd feared - skin inflamed, wounds already making an effort to clot. It wouldn't scar, unlike her hand. She would live with the repercussions of that injury for the rest of her life. I tried not to wonder how long that might be.

"We have to fix this. We have to stop her."

Snot rubbed off onto the shoulder of my sweater, courtesy of my sister. Nevertheless, I cradled her to me so closely that it was tough to tell where I ended and she began.

"We will." I dropped a kiss to her head; a pale imitation of Mom. "I won't let her get you."

The wail that rattled from Becca's chest was not so effortlessly soothed away, despite my rocking and the oaths I mumbled into her hair. I couldn't tell how long we had sat like that – entangled and falling apart – before Becca started trying to wiggle free, and I allowed her. Getting to my feet was more difficult than I'd anticipated since my left leg had gone to sleep and Becca, uninhibited by such an inconvenience, managed to escape the bathroom whilst I was hobbling around using the furniture to lean on.

"Becca! Wait!"

I traced her to her bedroom with ease given the noises coming from within. I toed the door open to the sight of carnage, presided over by my sister, who scurried around the room with a manic kind of purpose. She emptied drawers onto her bed with her one hand, then moved on from the mess after barely a glance, to sweep perfume bottles and stuffed animals off their shelves. For once, her hair – her crowning glory – stuck up all over at ridiculous angles. She looked crazed.

"What are you doing?"

There was more grunting and panting as Becca struggled to shove her bed away from the wall with her shoulder.

"Don't stand there, help me," she instructed. When I didn't move, she added, "They were under Charlie's bed. Maybe they're under mine."

It dawned on me, then. What she actually meant, and what she was doing. She was looking for yew berries, because Becca believed she had been marked.

I left my post at the door to dive straight in to helping. We checked under the bed, even under the mattress, tearing all the sheets off and throwing them into the hall to be sure. Once the bed was cleared, we proceeded to the dressers. Within minutes, we had them emptied, adding to the growing mound out in the hall. If Mom or Dad got back whilst we were in the middle of ripping Becca's room apart then we wouldn't need to worry about Agnes because they'd kill us first.

"Not here," mumbled Becca, wincing as her frown tugged at the infant cuts marring her face. "I don't understand."

Neither did I. The berries marking Charlie had indeed been under her bed - smashed into the carpet, to be specific - whilst Tiff had found hers in her coat pocket, and Rose's had been hidden away in her purse, like Jenny's. Did that mean that whoever controlled the witch had somehow accessed Charlie's room? Maybe they rolled out of her schoolbag when she'd tossed it under there? If it was the former, rather than the latter, then who was it that Charlie had allowed into her life that harboured such evil intent? Someone from class; *LostBoy666*; some other freak she'd met in that semi-secret life of hers, where she smoked cigarettes and got loaded? I didn't have an answer.

Becca squealed, and I whirled to watch whatever she gripped in her hand drop to the floor. We both hit our knees at the same moment. I foraged in the mess whilst Becca sat back on her butt, pulling her knees into her chest. When she started rocking, arms locked around her calves, I knew it wasn't good.

It took me seconds to find the pencil case. Becca always carried way too many pens and rarely could close the zip as a result. It bulged open, as usual, and yet rather than stationary, it was bright berries that peeked out from the gap.

My sister had been right. She was next.

5

DAY 11 – 09:23 HRS

We were both skipping school again. Becca, at least, had a valid reason, what with her hand and now her face. For me, school no longer felt important or necessary. What was the point when there was probably zero chance I'd get to sit end of year exams, to graduate, or to grow up?

I left for the bus in the morning after kissing Mom goodbye, then hid behind the library until Becca texted that our parents had left for work. That was when I doubled back and my sister let me in through the screen door in the yard, to circumvent our nosey neighbours.

I'd spent the previous night on Becca's floor in a sleeping bag since my window wouldn't be fixed for a while. As usual, our parents took our phones before bed, this time switching them off to secure some peace from the outside world. They'd noticed how quiet and withdrawn we were both becoming, and chalked it up to other students hounding us over the situation with Charlie and Tiff. We didn't bother denying or confirming anything. It felt safer to allow them to draw their own conclusions, just as they had over Becca's face. *She must have done it in her sleep*, Mom had declared as she looked over the healing scratches with a critical eye.

As soon as I turned my cell back on, it seized with an onslaught of missed call and text notifications. I knew at once they were all from Hayley. I'd let her down over visiting Rose without explanation. As it turned out, she had stuck to her word about not trying to be a hero. She stayed home with her parents, waiting for me, and I disappointed her. It was becoming a pattern of behaviour that I couldn't seem to buck.

I decided that Hayley was probably (justifiably) pretty exasperated with me, so I didn't bother reading her texts or listening to the voicemails. Once I was back home, hiding out, I deleted everything with a swipe of my thumb before I tapped out the most honest message I could stand to.

'We have 2 assume R is gone.'

Hayley fired back immediately, as if she'd been waiting.

'No. No giving up.'

I stared at the screen, irate at Hayley's insistence on being a good friend. It hadn't mattered to her out by the 'twisted tree' when she'd tried to pound Rose into the ground for bitching about Charlie.

'B found berries.' I hit send with unnecessary ferocity.

Three jumping dots appeared onscreen and I knew that Hayley was hammering out her reply, probably so shaken by my revelation that she was all thumbs.

'Shit. Still checking on R l8r.'

I groaned, head dropping against the wall I slumped against.

'Waste of time! Need 2 talk 2 LostBoy666.'

In my heart, I knew that Rose was gone. Her radio silence coupled with her absence from school was confirmation enough. Still, I felt rotten to the core for suggesting that we give up on her. I tried to repress my guilt over it by reminding myself that Becca was the one who needed help. If I could save my sister then nothing else should matter. It was a shrewd way of looking at things, but if the only shot I had of protecting Becca was to let go of friends who were probably already dead, then I was going to shoot it. Maybe, I thought, they would have understood.

My cell pinged and I looked down. It was hard to read through the tears of self-loathing brimming in my eyes.

'*Y? What can he do??*'

I would have thought it was obvious. I spelled it out for Hayley, regardless.

'*Maybe C + LB met. Maybe LB is the 1.*'

'*The 1?*'

I fidgeted, swallowed, and typed back.

'*Controlling Aggie.*'

My phone remained inert for a long time. So long, in fact, that I'd almost forgotten about the exchange with Hayley when it jerked. I'd been taking a leaf out of Mom's book, brewing coffee, since I hadn't slept undisturbed by nightmares and the echoes of a few days of solid trauma.

'*On it.*' It was enough of a promise, and I sighed in relief as I filled mugs for myself and Becca.

I'd given it a lot of thought; so much, in fact, that I'd already convinced myself of the truth of it. *LostBoy666* had to be the culprit. Charlie must have been meeting with him in secret, and who the hell knew what had transpired from there? Maybe she'd turned him down, maybe she'd insulted him, or maybe she hadn't needed to do a damn thing at all. Some people were born evil, after all, like Bundy, Gacy, and Ramirez. The history books and the news were full of their stories. Cautionary tales to humanity. Whatever the reason, I was sure *LostBoy* was the one who had woken Agnes and planted the berries on Charlie in the first place. The rest of us were collateral damage. We were all linked – from Mrs. Pedlow right through to Becca – and that couldn't be coincidence. This mystery internet guy, who ensnared Charlie with his wit and knowledge of the occult, had to be our perp. There was nobody else worth considering.

As I had lain awake the night before, listening out for Becca's deep breathing, I'd realised that trying to stop Agnes directly was the wrong approach. She was old, powerful, and beyond pissed off with the world: there was no conceivable way a bunch of teenagers could face that and win. Instead, we had to find out who was responsible for raising the witch and deal directly with them. I was going to take *LostBoy666* apart, piece by piece, until he put that bitch back in the ground.

Later in the afternoon, whilst Becca curled on the couch with a blanket and a movie, I lit some candles around the tub and drew myself a bath. Every bone in my body ached and every muscle throbbed as a consequence of some imagined exertion. Stress could have a weird effect on the body, I decided as I sank into the warm water and bubbles until I was submerged up to my collarbone.

I could hear the TV from downstairs. Becca always cranked the volume too high. Wild shrieking from whatever she was watching passed through the floorboards, uninhibited, making me wish I'd had the foresight to grab my radio. I amused myself listening to the garbled speech as I worked the soap into a lather from my wrists to my shoulders. Exhaustion forced me to lean my head back against Mom's bath pillow, and I allowed my sponge to float away towards my toes on the surface of the water as the heat worked its magic. Against my will, it lulled me into half-consciousness – to that place that exists between reality and fantasy, where the sounds of our world are stitched to visions from the next. A Frankenstein's monster of waking and sleeping thought. It's the same state of being that allows the alarm clock to bleed through into your best dreams of meeting your favourite band. You only realise that you're not really awake when they strike out on stage and the guitar solo resembles an incessant bleeping that won't quit. I had never experienced it like this before, though.

It was evident that the laughter circling Mum's Woods didn't belong. It was far too weird to be human yet not so sinister that I could pin it on Agnes. The dialogue that followed was equally out of place; circling around labyrinths, squalling babies, and goblin kings. Things had gotten bad at Mildenhall but they weren't quite that level of crazy.

I dug my bare toes into the ground to be rewarded with the crackle of fallen leaves desiccating under my weight. I must have slipped fully into unconsciousness at that point because the whistle of the wind picked up to replace the chorus of a jaunty song that didn't fit the scene. The chords faded into oblivion as I became fully immersed in the dream.

A streak in my peripheral vision drew me to the side of the old postal centre, where five figures gathered to wait. Charlie. Mrs. Pedlow. Tiff. Jennifer. Rose. Dominoes, in the order they had toppled.

They formed a line, silent and watchful. The robes they wore – chalk-white and flowing – emphasised the pallor of their skin, which had been kissed all over by the blatant mottling of death. Blue lips, cloudy eyes, nails caked in dirt, as though they had dug their way out of graves that didn't exist – they were a terrifying vision that I experienced with more clarity than I would have liked. I folded in on myself around a wounded cry.

I reached out with one hand. Charlie might have smiled at the offer or it might have been a trick of the light, courtesy of the midday sun that crested the treetops. None of them moved to meet me and, astonishingly, I was disappointed. Even in the state they were in, there was comfort, maybe closure, to be found in the brushing together of fingers, or the resting of a head upon a shoulder. I would have taken anything. What I received was nothing.

Charlie was the first to glide with ethereal elegance towards the mouth of Mum's Woods. The others followed like soldier ants, determined in their purpose. Against my will, I fell into step behind Rose, who kept her head bowed and her steps long as she worked to meet the pace that Charlie set. Only I breathed hard against it, the air rasping in and out of my lungs thanks to the punishing gait. Physical displays of exhaustion made everything seem more real and I debated pinching myself to dispel the nightmare, if only because it was too tangible. In the end, I decided against it. There had to be a reason for it - for me to be there, with them as they were, and I knew I owed it to my friends to stick around.

We stopped at the 'twisted tree', arriving so abruptly that I almost ran into the back of Rose. I couldn't help cringing when I saw the spread of blood on the robe between her shoulder blades. It looked fresh, like if I reached out my hand to touch it then my fingers would come away tacky. There was no doubt in my mind now that she was dead – like Charlie and the others – but the question of how it had happened niggled at me. It was difficult to consider that I might never know. After all, the cops had found no bodies, aside from Mrs. Pedlow.

I lined up beside my ghosts without fuss. When they turned inwards to the woods to face the tree with its malformed trunk, I copied. It took me a while to realise that a grave silence reigned over everything. That even the birds that cavorted overhead did so without the flap of beating wings. Branches jittered in a wind that no longer whispered, and I grew colder from the inside out as the sky darkened through every shade of afternoon to nightfall in an impossible hurtle of seconds. Gradually, the trunk of the tree unwound itself, like strands of rope fraying. It stood suddenly straight and true, branches pointing proudly to the sky. This change was marked by a scream.

Sound rushed back into my ears so fast that it was painful and unpleasant. I bit my tongue in the confusion so that the tart tang of blood flooded my mouth. *Odd for a dream*, I remember thinking, but that was all I managed before the bodies crashed through the trees.

Three men dragged a woman between them – one on each side to grip her underarm, and the last with his hand wound around the length of her red braid. It was unnecessarily cruel: she was limp in their arms anyway, chin touching her chest, and the ugly wound above her temple seemed to have sucked all the fight out of her. They pulled her as if she was a ragdoll, her head snapping so violently with the motion that I was shocked her neck didn't crack under the strain. The men spat at her feet and growled curses in her face, which they poked and slapped with calloused hands that worked the land as hard as they were working her.

She whimpered – a pitiful noise – but her captors were wilfully deaf to her distress. They tossed her to the floor, where she curled into the foetal position, her body shuddering enough that the rustle of her skirts against the leaves and moss was as audible as her moans. The rest of the villagers spilled into the clearing with less haste. The women hung back at the fringe of the mob, clutching shawls around their shoulders and blinking back tears that made their pupils gleam like devils in the moonlight. I expected to find joy written on their faces but all I could see there was despair; deep worn lines, downturned mouths, and sunken eyes. Whether they believed wholeheartedly in Agnes' guilt or not, it was clear that they were dissatisfied with their lot, and what woman wouldn't be? If they didn't point the finger at their mothers, their sisters, their daughters, their friends, they would find one instead pointing at them. To become the accuser or accused: there was no alternative.

"Agnes Tippett, ye be guilty of witchcraft, and of lying wi' the devil as his unholy whore."

Agnes recoiled and so did I, however, I wasn't the one to receive a boot to the gut in reprimand. She groaned, flopping onto her back as she coughed. The man who had kicked her hooted, although there was little humour in it. He eyed the young girl at his feet like she was a poisonous snake. To his mind, she was just as bad. A deadly viper waiting to strike. All I saw was a skinny, frightened teenager.

"Please, no... I swear... I..."

The boot landed a second time. Agnes couldn't find the breath to wail so I did it for her, whipping my head back around to seek out Charlie and the others. They were gone and I stood alone.

"Still your vile tongue, witch."

They left her in the dirt, spitting blood from a split lip, whilst they busied themselves snapping branches from the thickest of the nearby tress: the 'twisted tree', yet to earn its name.

When four branches were gathered, the men took out their knives to carve the tips to points that resembled spears. A dark patch of urine stained Agnes' skirts, though nobody noticed. She had given up pleading when the front of the crowd had started to pelt her with stones, making it clear that there'd be no leniency. It took five of them to pin her down once her panic took hold, and a sixth to drive the stakes home. He used his whole body and roared with the effort, consenting to smile when blood splattered the front of his white shirt. To the casual observer – to me – he enjoyed it.

Agnes howled until she passed out, which wasn't until the

third branch pierced above the kneecap of her right leg, shattering the bone on its way through to the ground. I watched it all, wishing I wasn't. They wandered away minutes after the deed was done, none of them sparing a glance for the girl they had ruined. I covered my face with my hands to wipe away the angry tears that had burned a path down my cheeks. When I raised my head, I found the sky awash with shades of muted orange and pink, and Agnes close to death amongst the bracken.

The vacancy in her eyes was telling. So was the way her mouth hung slack to allow the circling flies to land on her swollen tongue. The blood hadn't dried or stopped flowing, and Agnes' life was draining into the soil along with it. The roots of the once 'twisted tree' - stretched beneath the dirt on which her body lay - must have been drinking her in as nourishment. I felt sick, disgusted, outraged, having witnessed the crime that had been visited on this girl. And, yet, there was more to come.

He wafted between the tress like he was made of smoke. His footfalls were soundless. He wore smart black clothes and a tall hat with a wide brim, which somehow didn't disturb the branches he brushed as he made his way towards Agnes.

"Poor child," he crooned in a silken voice that forced Agnes' eyelids half open. *"Sweet lamb."*

He caressed her bloodied hair, her pale face, her limp hand, squatting there on the woodland floor beside her. A tear ebbed from her eye and he caught it with the sharpened nail of his thumb before he sucked it into his mouth. The scene was all kinds of wrong. The smile that curved his lips made it worse.

"I can help you." Agnes cried harder. *"I can ease your agony. You have only to say the word."*

Agnes nodded as best she could. Her strength was deserting her but I could see from the tautness of her muscles that the pain wasn't. Who could blame her for accepting such an offer?

There was no mistaking when Agnes' torment ended. It was

right when his palm pressed to her forehead. Her smile was small as she sagged against the ground, bottom lip trembling from a mixture of gratitude and anguish. She obviously knew she was done for - that this could be only a temporary reprieve. Regardless, she whispered her thanks to the stranger. Whoever he was, he was far from human, and I was beginning to catch glimpses of the pitch-black aura that outlined his form.

"It will not be long now, child." It wasn't a soothing statement yet it eased Agnes' turmoil a little. *"Will you allow me to help you one last time?"*

The next words he spoke were a mystery to me. He uttered them directly into the shell of Agnes' ear. I watched her shiver when his breath warmed her lobe, and I could tell that she wasn't enjoying the intimacy. He drew back after a moment and settled on his haunches to watch Agnes.

"No falsehoods. No tricks. I swear it upon my honour."

That smile, again. So perverse and wicked that I expected to see fangs when his lips peeled back to reveal his gums. It was the most predatory smile I had ever seen.

"You will rest," he said. A vow. *"When you wake, they shall pay for their sins."*

Maybe it was the light. I probably would have blamed that or my imagination or twenty other things before all of this had started. However, when his irises flashed crimson for a brief moment, I didn't doubt it.

To her credit, Agnes considered the proposition for a minute longer than most people in her shoes would have. Myself included. The desire for revenge is an all too human one. We can downplay it, try to deny it, but there's no changing the fact that when we're so viciously wronged, the idea of retribution is like a drug. We crave it as if it's the answer to all of our problems, then we stuff it inside of ourselves until we're so full of it that it overtakes everything. I watched Agnes do just that, sealing the deal with her helpful stranger with a kiss. She breathed her last breath as their lips parted.

Water filled my mouth, my eyes, my ears, my nose. Hands pinched at my slick skin to wrench me from underneath the suds, and I emerged hacking so hard that I vomited bile into the tub. I sucked in air in big, grateful gulps as soon as I was able.

"Olly! Shit, oh shit, I thought you'd drowned!"

Becca was already draping the towel around my shoulders before I'd managed to fall out of the bath. I landed on my knees on the mat and continued to cough until the last of the soapy water was purged from my body. Then, I collapsed against the side of the tub and allowed it to bear my weight, completely unbothered by my nakedness. More for her comfort than mine, Becca arranged the towel to protect what was left of my modesty.

"You fell asleep," she accused. Her pupils were blown so wide that her eyes were almost completely black. "I heard you thrashing around. If I hadn't come to check..."

She trailed off. There was genuine fear in her expression. I reached for her with a wet hand to pat her knee, doing all I could to comfort her though I hadn't put myself back together fully.

"I wasn't asleep. I saw Charlie and the others. I saw Agnes Tippet die."

"It was a dream because - like I said - you fell asleep!"

Squirming under my sister's reproach, I pulled the towel tighter around my body. The bath water was tepid and the droplets drying on my skin were starting to chill me. I pressed my nose into my fist, covered by the thick cotton, and rubbed my face against the towel. I used to do it all the time as a kid but it suddenly didn't bring me the same level of comfort as it used to.

"It wasn't a dream," I insisted. "It was a vision. Rose is dead. They're all dead."

I heard Becca swallow the lump in her throat and, despite still being mildly pissed at me, she scooted closer so that we could huddle together. She didn't call me psycho this time, or question my claims.

"What did you see?" she asked, eventually, in a tiny voice that barely piqued above the whir of the bathroom fan.

I told her everything, leaving nothing out, including the appearance of our friends and the more brutal details of Agnes' death. I'd almost finished relaying the scene to her when her cell phone kicked into life in her pocket. We both jumped and gripped each other more fiercely.

"It's from Hayley." Becca scanned the message, eyes narrowed, and she wordlessly passed her cell to me for inspection.

The name *LostBoy666* caught my eye first. It was a copy of an instant message Hayley had sent, plus the one she'd received in return. I straightened, dislodging Becca's head from where it rested on my shoulder as I brought the phone closer to my face. Hayley had reached out to Charlie's secret online boyfriend, after all. The response she'd received hadn't exactly been helpful.

I stared at the messages with laser focus, hard enough to incinerate the phone around which my fingers flexed. White hot fury pulsed through my body and seared my veins, sealing them off against the usual rush of blood. The tips of my extremities started to tingle and I forced myself to look away before staring at *LostBoy666*'s exhibition of casual cruelty pushed me over the edge.

I shoved the cell back at Becca. Whether I carried on reading and rereading the messages or not, their content was printed in my mind and probably on my retinas, too. His last words to Hayley – his only words, in fact – damned him as much as any straight up admission.

A single laughing face, then, the sentence that made me despise this boy more than I hated anyone. More than I even hated Agnes.

'Ur screwed... RIP, bitches.'

The berry emoji that proceeded was the icing on the cake.

6

DAY 11 – 17:26 HRS

Rose's parents kept a spare key taped to the bottom of the birdhouse in their front yard. The military housing company would have shit porcupines if they'd found out, especially since the Anderson quarter was off camp, but it wasn't like any of us would rat on them. Not when their propensity for locking themselves out of the house actually worked in our favour.

Hayley fished the key out of its hiding place and unlocked the door. Right as we filed inside, the telephone mounted to the kitchen wall started to ring, and I glanced at the others for direction.

"Leave it," Hayley ordered. "Rose's parents are away. Her mom is probably calling to check in on her."

"Shouldn't we talk to her? Let her know that Rose..."

A dark look flashed across Hayley's face and Becca stopped talking, intimidated.

"What would we say? 'Hey, Mrs. Anderson, we can't find your daughter, haven't seen her in days. Actually, we think she might have been murdered by a witch. We just broke into your house with the spare key, by the way. How's the trip?'"

It was a fair point. There was nothing we could say to Mrs.

Anderson that would help the situation, and worrying her when she was hundreds of miles away wouldn't achieve anything, except for bringing the cops down on our heads. We had already come to the conclusion that the police, and probably not even the military, could handle this. Specifically, they couldn't handle Agnes. That was, if they believed us in the first place. It was more likely that we'd be accused of hysteria and put under house arrest by our parents. Any hope we had of stopping the witch would be snatched away.

We let the phone ring out.

I'd been inside Rose's house a handful of times before so I wasn't as familiar with it as I was with the Hill home. Becca and I followed Hayley from room to room like two little ducklings whilst she searched for signs of Rose's recent presence. We found a couple of dirty plates on the coffee table and a pair of boots at the bottom of the stairs, but otherwise there were no signs that Rose or anyone had existed inside the house for days. I'd expected disarray; shattered windows, upturned furniture, claw marks raking the walls. Bloodstains. Instead, I got neatly arranged scatter pillows and bowls of potpourri. I decided the calm was a far more eerie beast to behold than chaos would have been.

We circled back to the kitchen, where we gathered at the table to conduct our war council. As it turned out, our next move was to order pizza since our stomachs had started to growl far too obnoxiously to ignore. Whilst Becca ordered online, Hayley pulled the pin from her latest grenade and tossed it into our midst.

"I found berries this morning. They were in the saddlebag on my bike."

My eyes narrowed to slits. Of course. Her bike was stored outside most of the year, leaning up against the garage, protected by a sheet of tarp when the weather got too bad.

Otherwise, it was easy to access for anyone who knew where the Hills lived. The perfect way to mark Hayley without having to get close.

She started to cry or, at least, she started to swipe at the tears as they beaded on her lashes. I made to grab for her hand but Hayley stepped away from me to press her back against the kitchen cupboards. She lowered her head so that I couldn't watch her too closely whilst she fought to regain her composure.

"Are you sure?" Becca set her phone on the table, order complete, and shifted her focus to the more pressing matter.

"Positive."

When Hayley raised her face, her mask of calm was back in place. The only indication that she had been upset was the slight flush to her cheeks.

"We'll work this out." I was doing a good job selling the confidence I didn't feel. "We'll fix this before anything happens to you or Becca."

"I'm not sure it matters anymore," said Hayley, despondent. "Charlie's gone. Tiff is gone. Rose is probably gone, too. What's left to fight for?"

Triggered by her words, maybe also by her distress, I pulled back my shoulders to lift my head high.

"You, me, and Becca. *We're* worth fighting for. The others would never have wanted us to give up." There was steel in my voice; cold and unbending – a warning that I wasn't willing to compromise on this - to wave the white flag and submit. After everything that *LostBoy* and Agnes had taken from us, it would be an incomprehensible choice to make.

"She's right. If we're going down then at least let's go down swinging."

I nodded in agreement with Becca, so proud of the way she straightened her spine and squared her jaw. We waited for Hayley's decision whilst she examined her shoes, giving nothing away in the line of her pressed lips or the empty look in her eyes. Although I could understand how exhaustion and fear and grief could snowball into the overwhelming urge to surrender, the idea was against my nature. I wanted to live – wanted my sister and my friend to live, too. There'd been enough death at Mildenhall already without conceding to become a body on a slab. We deserved better than that.

"Okay." Hayley spoke on the conclusion of a sigh. It didn't matter. I had the answer I'd wanted and I wasn't going to give her the chance to change her mind.

"I have something I need to tell you, too. I know what really happened to Aggie. I saw it all."

I poured out the story of Agnes and her death as Becca raided the cabinets for plates and Hayley stared at me in varying measures of disbelief. She interjected with questions sporadically but mostly I got to tell the tale through, finishing on the doorbell chime. I went to grab the pizza from the delivery guy, leaving Hayley to recover and Becca to fill our water glasses with her good hand. It was tough staggering back under the boxes of wings, pizza, and garlic bread, and I had to stop to readjust the load a couple of times before I actually made it to the door. I must have moved silently enough because neither Becca nor Hayley heard me approach, which was pretty obvious given the subject matter of their hushed conversation. Mom always hated it when I eavesdropped. It was a habit I'd developed as a young kid and hadn't managed to break, though I could admit to not putting in much work there. Intrigued by the vitriol in Becca's tone, I paused, leaning my shoulder against the wall so that the boxes were partially supported.

"All I'm saying is, don't you think it's weird that Olly didn't get any berries? Why Mrs. Pedlow? Why Jennifer? What did they do to piss off *LostBoy*? How did he even get to them? This doesn't add up, Becca. Why would it be some random guy off the internet who may or may not have been having a relationship with Charlie?"

Becca was quick to bite back, hackles raising with her instinctive desire to protect me. "You saw his message. You contacted him yourself. Are you accusing my sister now or something?"

"No. I'm not accusing anyone of anything. I'm asking the questions that you don't seem to want to. Why does Olly get to be the one who walks away from all this?"

"I can't believe you actually think she would summon the witch. That's insane. I mean, she didn't believe in stuff like this until Charlie disappeared."

"So she said. And now she's having visions of Agnes Tippet? Kind of a huge coincidence, if you ask me."

"She's not a liar." Becca's voice rose and I wondered if I should burst into the kitchen to diffuse the brewing row. Something held me back. Call it morbid curiosity, perhaps, but I suddenly had to know if my sister and my one remaining friend suspected I could be capable of such heinous things.

"I'm not implying that," soothed Hayley. My fingers clenched around the boxes and I bit down on my lip, sealing my mouth closed against the growl that rumbled in my chest. She definitely wasn't implying anything positive.

"Whatever. I know my sister. She wouldn't," Becca said, loyal to a fault yet still somewhat tentative. My heart sank at the wavering note in her voice that made her next statement come off sounding more like a question. "She couldn't?"

I remained in the corridor, breathing fast, as my ears strained to detect the rest of the conversation.

"I'm sorry. I'm just scared. Forget I said anything, okay?"

Deciding I'd heard enough, I strode into the kitchen, brandishing our dinner and a smile, and pretending like I hadn't covertly witnessed my own character assassination. Hayley, having the decency to look regretful, hid behind the need to drain all the water from her glass, and I let her. It was better not to challenge her - to pretend I'd heard nothing rather than to start something and risk driving a wedge between the three of us when we were relying on each other for survival. She didn't mean it, I assured myself, only partially believing it. Even if she did, sticking together was imperative if I was going to save my sister. There was safety in numbers, and ours were dwindling at an astounding rate these days.

I could admit that Hayley had a point about one thing, though: it was a mystery to me also as to why *LostBoy* had decided that I was going to be the one spared. I would have surely been a more obvious choice than either Mrs. Pedlow or Jennifer, who Charlie wouldn't have had much cause to discuss with him. I tried to tell myself that it wasn't important - that whether it was a random decision or a conscious one rooted in some skewed logic - it didn't alter the situation. Irrespective, the thought niggled as I reached for the plate that Becca nudged across the table. She didn't, or couldn't, meet my eyes and the enormity of that decimated my appetite. Mostly for show, I placed a single slice of pizza on my plate and nibbled on a chicken wing.

We picked at our food in silence, which wasn't characteristic for any of us. My friends and I liked to eat, and I don't mean undressed salads and rice crackers. None of that wannabe supermodel crap. We were all about s'mores around the campfire, sticky barbecue ribs on game days, and loaded fries at the diner. As soon as I was struck by the realisation that Charlie, Tiff, and Rose would never get to taste chocolate or Chinese food or greasy diner lunches again, it was all I could do to keep from wailing. I shoved my plate aside and forced down some water, hoping to put out the fire of despair I'd lit in my belly.

"What are we going to do about Agnes?"

Hayley and I looked up, eyes clashing unintentionally for a second before we both turned to Becca. My sister hunched over the table, her uninjured hand, which rested palm up on the surface, sticky with tomato sauce. Most of her pizza remained on the plate, though, torn into bite-size chunks.

"We could go back to the museum. Maybe that guide we spoke to could help us?" I suggested.

To my surprise, Becca scoffed and rolled her eyes. I tried not to take it personally or to allow the new paranoia I had developed to fester.

"Or maybe he'll think we're playing a prank on him. Or worse, maybe he'll think we're sick in the head, and we'll end up sitting in straightjackets when Aggie comes for us."

I bristled, unaccustomed to such real hostility from my baby sister. Sometimes we fought, like all families do, but it was usually over fast, and we never cut each other deep with our words or actions.

"You think of something, then."

"I'd love to, but right now my brain is too busy processing my certain death to be top of its game. Sorry to inconvenience you."

"What the hell, Becca? Why are you being such a bitch?"

"Oh, I don't know. Could have something to do with the rancid hag that's planning on murdering me. Not like that's a problem you have to worry about..."

"If you have something to say to me..."

A fist slammed down on the table. The plates and water glasses jumped at the abrupt contact and so did we, however, neither Becca nor I were willing to be the first to back down. We continued to glower and snarl at each other.

"That's enough! Do you think this is helping?" demanded Hayley. A hand drifted to her popped hip, making her look like a mom taking her kids to task. "You two don't realise how lucky you are to have each other."

I reeled, leaning away from the table and clutching a fist to my stomach. Becca managed to look both simultaneously devastated and embarrassed. She dropped her gaze to her bandages, which were coming unravelled after Mom had done a poor job of replacing them earlier in the day. I made a mental note to offer my help when they came due again, if only to keep my sister from contracting sepsis or some other deadly infection. The self-inflicted scratches on her face didn't look nearly as severe in the light of day, and she'd been able to pass those off as accidental to anyone who'd asked.

"I'd give anything to be able to talk to Charlie," Hayley paused, collecting herself with a deep, stuttering breath, "so quit yelling at each other and get it together! If we don't stop Agnes then my sister's death was for nothing, and I can't live with that."

We mumbled our apologies first to Hayley and then swiftly to each other, although Becca couldn't quite meet my eyes when she spoke. That brought a pang of sadness to me that resonated deep inside the cavern of my chest, which already felt hollow. Like a void. Truthfully, I was beginning to worry that my heart had shrivelled away into nothing, unable to withstand so much loss.

"I guess we need a more solid plan."

It was the only indication of relenting that Becca was willing to give. For me, there was nothing else to do but nod in agreement with her. My well had run dry, and I was all out of ideas when it came to how to deal with either Agnes or *LostBoy*. There was no way of knowing who he was, where he was hiding, or what his next move was to be, which ruined any chance of finding him and somehow forcing him to end Agnes' reign of terror. Just as *LostBoy* had predicted, we were screwed.

"What if we destroy the tree?"

I blinked, confused, at Hayley, who stood in the middle of Rose's kitchen with her feet planted shoulder-width apart and her brow creased in concentration. When neither of us replied or moved in any way to acknowledge her, Hayley cleared her throat harshly. We couldn't help but look then, and she waited for our full attention before she went on.

"You said that the tree was in your dream, Olly."

"Vision," I corrected, reflexively.

"Vision," Hayley amended, keen to continue minus further interruption. "The legend mentions the tree and so does Agnes' rhyme: that means it's got to be important somehow. Olly saw that thing change, right? You said it was a regular tree before Agnes died."

I nodded, all the finer details of the vision so clear in my mind; Agnes' flaming hair fanned out against the bracken; the branches stripped from the tree, then whittled to lethal points; the blood that had soaked beneath the soil as if suckled by the yew itself.

"You're right. Agnes has to be tied to the 'twisted tree'."

I couldn't say with any confidence that Agnes had been buried there, as lore and legend claimed. But - regardless of whether the witch was interred at Mum's Woods or not - she was a part of that land, ingrained within it through the sweat, tears, and blood she had shed upon it. They were one and the same, bound to each other, and forged together for the rest of time. What Hayley was insinuating suddenly started to make a lot more sense.

"Maybe if we destroy that tree, we destroy Aggie, too. They used to burn witches, right? So let's torch that mother and finish her off for good."

The three of us observed each other in silence, stewing for a while in Hayley's proposal, which was really the only one we had. Even if there had been others, perhaps this still would have made the most sense.

"How do we know it'll work?" Becca asked as she played with the end of her bandage and avoided looking at us both.

"We don't," came the answer, which opened a gully in my stomach so vast that I feared it might never close. "But you were the ones telling me a few minutes ago that we have to try."

She had us there. One glance at Becca confirmed it.

"We could go tomorrow," I suggested. "We know when the guards patrol, and where, so all we have to do is time it right."

Hayley flashed me a smile of encouragement.

"Go in, burn the tree, and get out before anyone has a chance to notice the flames."

It sounded simple in theory yet it would be risky, what with the heightened patrols the military police and guards had been conducting since Charlie had gone missing. I had no doubt, though, that the three of us were familiar enough with the geography of the base to pull it off. Besides, it wasn't exactly a complex plan, although that would work in our favour when attempting to execute it.

"What do you think, Becca?"

Hayley voiced the question I could not when the shadow of our recent row loomed so large over us.

Once, when I was nine and Becca was six, I'd stolen her favourite doll and hacked off most of its hair under the guise of playing salons. Really, I'd been pissed off that Becca had started gymnastics classes and learned to turn a better cartwheel than I could. I'd wanted to hurt her for the injustice and, to my childish mind, the wilful destruction of her property was the best way. My sister had been so enraged that she'd refused to look at me for three days straight. Eventually, the gravity of losing my favourite playmate had caught up with me, crushing me like a lonely avalanche, and I had gone to Becca sobbing for forgiveness. I couldn't recollect a time since when we had given each other the silent treatment - the ultimate slight in 'girl world'.

Now, though, the idea was growing more appealing. It was a terrible, hurtful thing to consider that my sister didn't trust me. I ached to lash out and inflict the same kind of wound upon her, so that she might understand it. Instead, I stayed quiet and tried not to glower too much.

"I'll bring the matches."

It was settled. All we had to do was survive twenty-four hours, then we could bring the whole nightmare to an end. That kind of thing nearly always worked in the movies that Charlie loved to watch as we lounged across her bed and tossed popcorn into each other's mouths. Then, once Aggie was out of the picture for good, we could work on a way to deal with *Lost-Boy666* before he could ruin any more lives.

We waited around for a half hour longer. It was impossible to remain optimistic that Rose might stroll through the front door like she didn't have a worry in the world. We all knew she was never coming back to that house. To her family. To us.

Before we left, Hayley washed the dishes whilst I dumped the leftovers in the neighbour's outside trash and Becca wiped down the table. We were careful to make sure we didn't leave so much as a crumb or a smear of grease behind, aware that it wouldn't look good for us all if anyone discovered we'd been eating take out in Rose's kitchen when she was missing. It would be a matter of time before her mom became concerned enough to come looking, or the school called to check on Rose's absence with her dad. It would be better if we couldn't be linked to another lost girl.

We remembered to return the spare key to its nook after we locked the door. Leaving the house in the perfect darkness in which we'd found it, we stole down the path, keeping to the shadows of the lawn to avoid being spotted by the rest of the street. The realisation that Rose was unquestionably gone stalked us all the way back to the corner of Washington Square, where we said goodbye to Hayley before watching her disappear into her house. We didn't budge until the door closed behind her. We needed that assurance.

For the first time in a long time that night, Becca and I exchanged glances. We both nodded, then we booked it to our house faster than either of us had been motivated to move before. I was breathing heavily when I reached the yard but I didn't fumble with my keys and, though I was mad at Becca, I shoved her into the hall ahead of me.

Soon as my foot touched down on the carpet, I felt better: safer, calmer, more in control. I lingered on the stoop – one foot in, one half out – whilst I took a moment to peer out. In a few days it would be Halloween, and the square would be alive with glowing, grinning jack-o-lanterns and costumed kids swinging their candy buckets. It had all been homely and welcoming to me once. Now, it was transformed in my mind into the Labyrinth. Behind every tree, garbage can, and shrub lurked the possibility of the monster. The difference was, the creature of legend we feared was no melancholy, misunderstood Minotaur, but a woman - beaten and scorned - who would stop at nothing in her quest.

The evening air coaxed a shudder from me so I took that as my cue to close the door. Without a second thought, I fastened every lock, bolt, and chain affixed to it, determined to shut out the enemy. If only I could have kept it that way, I might have spared us all more heartache, and the coming devastation that none of us could have foreseen.

In that single moment, though, the night was silent and still.

7

DAY 12 – 16:33 HRS

Coach Rhodes must have called in sick because I had an unexpected free period at the end of the day instead of mandatory gym class. I used the time to watch over my sister, sitting guard in the corridor outside French whilst I waited for school to let out. We hadn't left each other alone for more than twenty minutes since the conversation in Rose's kitchen. Even though there'd been conflict between me and Becca, we squashed our mutual irritation the best we could. Whatever issues had risen between us could be resolved once Agnes was a distant, unpleasant memory and the 'twisted tree' was a pile of ash. I couldn't have cared less if the fire we planned on setting took the whole woodland with it. I was becoming more and more convinced that only evil would come from that place.

The moment Becca swept out of her classroom, we fastened ourselves together and made for the bus waiting in the yard. Hayley had saved us seats on the back row. We didn't discuss our plans for the evening. If anyone had overheard, it would have been over before it had begun, and we weren't willing to risk the only plan we had falling flat because of some nosey junior who couldn't mind their own business.

About half way home, the downpour started. We exchanged looks that were fraught with worry. There was no way we would be able to get a fire going in such miserable weather - no matter how much fuel we splashed around. Immediately, Becca occupied herself checking the online forecast on her phone whilst I peered glumly at the torrents of water collecting in the potholes in the tarmac. The bus tyres sluiced through a puddle, spraying water at a couple of pedestrians and soaking them through. I watched out the rear window as one of them flipped the bird at the driver, who likely hadn't noticed the rain, let alone his mistake. 'Bill the Bus' - as we called him - had a particular way of looking at us kids as we alighted the steps each morning and afternoon: that look let us know that he was dead inside, and had been for some time. He completed his route seemingly on another plane of existence, but he gave us no trouble, as long as we returned the favour.

"It'll be over in about an hour or so," said Becca, raising her eyes from her screen. Somewhere from the front, a girl squealed and a gang of boys burst into laughter.

"That could work. We can wait a while."

I nodded at Hayley, agreeing, although we didn't have much choice in the matter. Becca slid her phone back into her bag, and we remained mute for the rest of the ride. The rain got steadily worse.

For once, Mom was waiting for us at home. She'd really been making an effort to be around more since Becca's 'accident'. She'd reduced her hours at work for the foreseeable future, and she'd been talking to Dad about booking some kind of vacation once Becca's hand was completely healed. I didn't want her to feel like we weren't grateful for that.

We sat with Mom for a while, talking through our day and pretending not to be paralysed with fear. All the while, Becca and I watched the clock above the stove like prisoners scheduled for execution. Noticing how distracted we seemed, Mom made numerous attempts at excavating the truth.

"What's the matter with you two? You're so squirelly."

"Nothing. We're fine. Right, Olly?"

I hadn't been listening, too busy frowning at the minute hand on the wall clock, which I swore was inching backwards. When I didn't answer fast enough, Becca kicked me under the table.

"Yeah. Fine," I said, forcing a smile as I discreetly rubbed my shin. If my sister hadn't been injured already, I would have kicked her back, harder.

"I told you both, you can talk to me about anything." Mom pursed her lips, not really angry but perhaps disappointed. "I won't judge you – either of you – no matter what it is."

I said nothing. I'd already expended most of my energy watching out for Becca and Hayley, and I was trying to conserve what was left for the task to come. I didn't have the reserves to deal with Mom's well-meaning probing, and so I took the coward's way out; I looked to Becca, indicating that I was leaving the damage control to her this time.

"I promise that we're okay, Mom." She dug deep and emerged with a convincing smile that I had to give her props for. "It's been crazy lately with everything going on around here but we're trying our best to put that all behind us. It's just going to take some time."

Mom leaned across the table with her arms outstretched and we each extended a hand to meet her desperate grasp. Her bottom lip trembled as she no doubt thought of our missing friends, who she had known and loved almost as long as we had. Through her friendships with their parents, Tiff, Charlie and Hayley had become her surrogate children by default. Not to mention that everybody naturally looked out for each other at Mildenhall, maybe more so than they had at any of the bases we had lived at in America. It was something about the trans-Atlantic transplant, I assumed. We were all foreigners here, on equal footing to each other, no matter what our roots back home consisted of.

"I'm proud of you girls."

Becca's smile widened. I didn't think it was so fake anymore. Mom never awarded praise insincerely and so, when we received it, it was all the more sweet to bask in.

"We're proud of you, too." I found myself whispering, eyes filling with tears I couldn't sniff back. "You and Dad. We got pretty lucky with you guys."

Although it was true, I'd never felt the urge to say it before. Suddenly, it seemed important. There was no way to tell how the night would pan out, or whether burning the tree would have any effect on Agnes at all. If the worst happened, and we succumbed to the curse on Mum's Woods, I wanted to make sure that our parents – the people who mattered – knew exactly what they meant to us. Charlie, Tiff, and Rose had never gotten the same chance. Unfortunately, our impromptu heart-to-heart with Mom made her more reluctant to see us leave when the rain eventually stopped.

"Can't you stay home tonight?" she pleaded – so unlike her, who valued the sense of independence she'd worked hard to instil in us. "I have a bad feeling."

Maybe there was something to be said for maternal instinct, I thought, as I dragged Mom in for a hug.

"We'll be at the diner," I assured her. "We're going to plan a prayer vigil for Charlie and Tiff."

I could see from the knit of her brow that she was dubious, although reluctant to forbid an activity as wholesome as a prayer vigil. She teetered on the edge of indecision, and that was when Becca swooped in to rescue the situation.

"Hayley is coming with us. We'll stick together and walk each other home. Pinkie promise."

Mom said nothing, however, the nod she gave was all the permission we needed. Before we ducked out of the door – quickly, so that she couldn't change her mind – I planted a kiss on her cheek that I hoped could communicate everything that the words lodged in my throat couldn't. If something went wrong, this could be the last time I saw my mom. Mindful of the same, Becca leaned in for an embrace that lasted several seconds longer than she normally would have allowed. When she drew back from it, Mom didn't look like she had wanted to let go. There was trepidation written in her expression, and wisps of fear dancing in her eyes.

We left hand in hand. If Mom thought it strange, she kept that to herself. Perhaps she was glad that we had anchored ourselves to each other. Perhaps it filled her with a false sense of security. Safety in numbers was the mantra we had been living by lately but it hadn't done much for Rose. If Agnes wanted to take us all, it would be as easy for her as stomping on ants.

Hayley waited at the bottom of the street, near the library, with a plastic gas bottle in one hand. She shook it at us and I heard liquid slosh around inside.

"This was all Dad had in the garage. It should be enough. Probably."

"I got the matches," said Becca, patting her bulging jacket pocket. "Let's do this."

The sidewalk was pocked with puddles of varying depths, which we skirted around instead of splashing through. The glow from the streetlights shone back at us on the surface of the water, drawing us in as if we were moths. I walked shoulder to shoulder with Hayley whilst Becca brought up the rear. My attention flitted from every dark alley that we passed to each copse of bushes, to the parked cars that lined the streets. Anywhere that someone - or *something* - might be able to hide.

When the wind picked up unexpectedly and began to caress the backs of our necks, my shoulders stiffened. I stopped walking so suddenly that Becca ran into the back of me and stepped on the heels of my boots.

"What..." Hayley started, only to be cut off by the hand I waved in her face.

I scanned the darkness in earnest, searching for the source of the faint whispers carried on the wind.

"Aggie. Aggie. Aggie. Aggie."

I saw it. A face glaring up at me from a nearby puddle. A face I had seen before, in a vision of the past. Agnes Tippet. The Mum's Wood witch.

She leered from the mirror-like surface, her hair in wild disarray about her face. Her skin - pale as death - was cracked and scored in texture, like the bark of a tree. When she grinned, she revealed rows of canine teeth, and I pushed back against Becca as fear took hold of me.

"Look," I choked out and they both did, issuing gasps that told me we all saw the same thing.

"She knows."

A hand reached for mine and I blindly took it. Becca's grip was clammy and fierce.

"Keep walking. Just keep walking," urged Hayley. She grabbed my elbow and shook me, trying to rouse me. *Stick to the plan*, I reminded myself, as Agnes snapped her jaws.

"It's a vision. She can't hurt us," Becca insisted.

She couldn't have been more wrong.

Clinging to each other, the three of us tucked our heads down and walked on. We moved faster this time, not that it did us much good. When we reached the next puddle that bejewelled the sidewalk, Agnes stared at us from within. I shot a glance back, finding the previous puddle devoid of anything but the muted reflection of the streetlights. Ignoring the witch, I continued a few paces until I was forced to stop or else wade through a third, much larger puddle. Agnes was there, too, gnashing those animalistic teeth. Becca made a noise of distress whilst Hayley took charge and encouraged us to skirt around, her fingers pinching our arms as she manoeuvred us.

And so it continued – on and on and on - until Aggie was throwing her head back and howling with laughter. The images of her shimmered and rippled, the puddles eddied by the occasional splatter of raindrops falling from trees and posts. Each time we encountered her, she appeared more unhinged than the last and we grew increasingly afraid, though we tried our best not to show it.

"Almost there."

Breathing erratically, Hayley shoved and tugged some more. I managed to wrench my attention from Aggie to refocus it on the horizon, where I found the old postal centre looming. All we had to do was cross the parking lot and we'd be at the edge of the woods, where we'd struggle to find puddles forming amongst the pine needles and trailing ivy. Agnes would be unable to follow.

I squeezed my sister's hand and she responded by returning the pressure. With our eyes fixed on our destination, the three of us broke into a sprint, towards the path that would lead us into the woods and away from the monster.

We didn't make it.

The puddle should have been harmless - barely twelve inches wide and not a centimetre deep - yet it wasn't. It exploded upwards at impossible height, showering us with a spray of muddy water that obscured my view. Hayley tumbled, landing on her rear, though she didn't waste time before she took to scrambling back across the concrete. Becca released a piercing scream that rattled in my ears, but didn't move – terror rendering her immobile. I could only stare with saucer-eyes at the witch, who had burst forth from the puddle as though it had served her as a doorway between worlds. She was so much bigger than I had expected, easily three times the size of the girl she had been. She crouched low to the ground on four elongated limbs that were jointed the wrong way and still run through with yew branches. Her torso swung parallel to the ground, hanging in balance like the swollen abdomen of a spider. Her neck had twisted one hundred and eighty degrees, which allowed her to face the right direction but looked horrendously painful. Red hair, once thick and lush, dangled like greasy rats-tails against ashen cheeks that were patched with moss. She opened her mouth to shift her jaw left to right, producing a click-clack sound in the process. She followed with a deliberate growl as her beady-eyes focussed in on us: her quarry.

The tatters of material that had once formed her dress and apron streamed from her in ribbons, leaving nothing of her deformed body to the imagination. However, Agnes didn't seem to care about modesty. In fact, Agnes didn't seem to remember what it was to be human. Everything about her was petrifying. Grotesque. A perversion.

And she was going to kill us.

8

DAY 12 – 19:14 HRS

"Run!"

I didn't need to be told twice. I grabbed for Becca's sleeve so that I could haul her along behind me. She outpaced me in a matter of seconds yet I clung on tight to her, reversing the roles and letting her tow me instead. We swerved towards the postal centre as opposed to the woods, where we would be unsure of our footing in the dark. Hayley managed to overtake us both but my feelings of relief at seeing her safe were short-lived when she stumbled and the gas bottle slid out of her hand. It thumped the tarmac and bounced before landing on its side beneath the beam of a streetlight.

Hayley carried on without it, too scared to correct her mistake, and I truly couldn't blame her. However, without fuel, it would be impossible to get the damp bark to light, and burning the tree had become imperative with Agnes on our asses. Without thinking, I released Becca to pull away from the herd. I didn't look back at them but I could tell from their frantic shouting that they'd stopped to see what the hell I was doing. Whilst Agnes thundered along on her damaged limbs, I raced for the gas. Eyes narrowed, the witch diverted her course to intercept mine.

I beat her to the prize - sliding home like a baseball player reaching the plate – and managed to snag the handle of the bottle before Aggie could reach me. She tottered drunkenly, head swaying and bobbing with the movement as if it were on a spring, and attempted to lunge from a crouched position. Her jaws passed so close to my face that her foul saliva splashed my cheek, and I grimaced as it dribbled across my skin. Agnes roared, closer to my ear than I would have liked, so I kicked out with my right leg and managed to clip her ankle. The blow sent the witch crashing to the ground, and Becca whooped in triumph whilst I leapt to my feet to resume running.

"Hurry!"

I clutched the bottle tighter, legs pumping to the point of aching as I covered ground. My sister screamed again and that was all the warning I had before the creature soared over my head. She squatted in front of me, barring my path, and I backed up a couple of paces on unsteady legs. My head whipped side to side as I searched for an escape route.

"Hey, Agnes! Over here! Come on! This way!"

Both Aggie and I turned in unison to stare at Hayley, who danced around the parking lot with her arms waving madly above her head. Agnes chittered like an overgrown cockroach and took a lumbering, undecided step away from me.

"No..." I whispered, although I had already lost Aggie's attention.

"Hayley, don't," warned Becca whilst Hayley continued to leap around, splashing through puddles and kicking her legs. She looked more like she was practicing for a new routine, though her movements lacked grace.

"Go!" Hayley bellowed, features setting. Then, she bolted back in the direction of the library. Agnes tore after her without giving me a second glance. Suddenly, I was no longer the more entertaining option.

It was only a temporary reprieve, I knew, but it was the chance that Becca and I needed to get out of the open. We raced towards the postal centre and ducked around the rear of the building. I pressed my back and shoulders to the wall, and tried not to dwell on Mrs. Pedlow, who had become Agnes' second victim mere feet away. If I'd allowed my mind to wander then I would have been able to picture her, prone and cold, lying with her head twisted almost clean off.

Becca's hand slid against mine. I peered sideways at her through the debilitating darkness, unable to make out anything amongst the shadows except for the outline of her body.

"We need to get to the tree." I nodded despite the fact she couldn't see me.

A bloodcurdling shriek jolted through me, blowing my pupils wide, and I squeezed Becca's hand so aggressively that she squeaked. All I could think of was Hayley, and how much trouble she had landed herself in for my benefit.

Keeping low to the ground, we made our way around the building, sliding our palms against the brick to guide us. The lights were out inside the postal centre and the streetlights didn't extend to the back of the building so our course was steered by a sliver of moonlight and a smattering of stars.

"There's a window open somewhere round here. I saw it when we were walking up earlier."

In that moment, I was overwhelmingly grateful for negligent postal workers.

The sound of Agnes keening alerted us to her presence before she barrelled around the corner, talons leaving pock marks in the concrete. Hayley was nowhere to be seen. I didn't allow myself time to consider what that could have meant.

"Here!"

I turned to follow Becca's voice in time to watch her legs disappear through the window cut half way into the wall. It was a sliding frame, which had been left hanging open. There was a dull thunk as Becca touched down on the other side. Eager to get away from Aggie, I dived headfirst after my sister. When I hit the floor, I was glad that there was a thick carpet to soften the landing. Somehow, I still managed to ram my shoulder into the edge of a desk, hard enough to bruise.

We hunkered on the floor for a few seconds as the fire escape door rattled on its hinges. Either Agnes had seen us make our escape or else she could sense us, because the witch battered the door over and over until I was sure that it wouldn't hold up against the assault.

"Hide!" I hissed to Becca, and we both scrambled to our feet. I clutched onto the gas bottle like a drowning man clings to a life preserver.

Becca led the way down the hall that separated the back offices from the counter, bending double to avoid being seen through the windows lining the outer wall. Every slam and thump that Aggie created reverberated back at us from the stone floor. When those echoes were accompanied by the ominous sounds of splintering wood and screeching metal, I immediately straightened. Reaching for Becca's elbow with my free hand, I raced down the remainder of the hall to burst through the door at the end of it a fraction of a second before Agnes emerged from the offices.

Becca and I found ourselves on the wrong side of the kiosk, faced by a row of stools and a transparent screen that ran from the top of the counter to the ceiling. It sealed the customer area off completely from the workers' desks, and I stood in blind panic for a moment as I realised we had trapped ourselves. I could hear the soles of Agnes' bare feet and the palms of her hands slapping the corridor floor, and I knew she would be close behind us. Whilst Becca examined the screen, I wedged the back of a stool under the door handle. It was a pathetic, futile move, given that Agnes had ripped the fire escape out, but at least I was doing something.

"Olivia!"

I turned to Becca right as Agnes roared then slammed against the barricaded door. The legs of the stool squealed as they slid against the floor and I shot a despairing look at my sister. Becca ran to the counter to duck beneath it, and I followed her since the alternative meant waiting for the monster to break through behind me.

"Got it!" I watched with a swell of relief as a half door cut into the wooden counter swung open. We would have to crawl through but it would bring us out onto the store side of the post office, where we stood a better chance of finding a way back to the street.

I ushered Becca ahead of me and she scuttled on her hands and knees through the hatch. Agnes bayed, frustrated, and continued to use her body as a battering ram. I picked up the pace, motivated by her frustration. I'd hardly made it into the front of the post office when the door flew out of the jamb. It had snapped in half – as clean and easy as a toothpick – and both pieces ricocheted so hard off the plastic window that it was almost ripped out of its fixings.

We dashed for the main door whilst Agnes mounted the counter - too big to have any hope of following us through the hatch. Instead, she alternated between pummelling the screen with her hands and feet. She was driven insane by her need to get to us - completely and utterly, teeth-snapping, claw-slashing berserk. It was a sight to behold but we didn't stop to take it in. Aggie head butted the window, leaving a smear of black, congealed blood behind, then the first cracks started to appear.

"Shit! Shit! Crap!"

A waterfall of expletives tumbled from Becca's mouth and she otherwise froze to stare at the witch, who rammed her face into the screen a second time. The bridge of Aggie's nose busted open but she didn't seem to feel it. She growled and went right back to driving her head against the window. I tugged on the door handle in desperation. I hadn't really expected it to give, nevertheless, I was still filled with disappointment when I met resistance. The lock mechanism clicked - barely audible over the ruckus Aggie was creating - and I was forced to accept that there was no way we'd be opening that door without a key.

"Olly, here!"

I followed Becca's cry to a window adjacent to the counter, which had been partially concealed from view by a shelf of packing boxes. I tapped my knuckles against it experimentally, relieved to find that a single pane of glass was all that separated us from the outside world. It was a narrow frame and it would be a tight squeeze but, if we were able to find something to break the window, we could make it.

Before I had the chance to look around, Becca was coming towards me with a metal stanchion in her arms. I met her halfway down the aisle to help shoulder the load, however, she waved me away. The bandage on her hand was working loose and the tail flapped with the movement.

"Back up, now!" my little sister ordered, and I stepped aside as she wielded the base of the pole.

She drove it into the window three times before the glass buckled then smashed. An alarm started to blare around us. I used my arm, protected by my winter jacket, to sweep away the jagged shards from the edge of the frame, before I motioned for Becca to climb through. I was right behind her, refusing to spare a glance for Aggie, who was staggering around behind the kiosk, clutching her ears and crashing into furniture. The burglar alarm wailed on, driving her over the brink of insanity, and I almost felt sorry for her.

"We have to get to the tree. You got the gas?"

I nodded at Becca, too winded to speak, and shook the bottle. Looking relieved, she offered me her hand and I clung to it. We made for the treeline with Agnes' screams and the postal centre alarm haunting us. My heart beat so fast that I could feel it in my throat, along with the bile that had started to pool there right around the time Agnes had shown up.

Reaching the 'twisted tree' was difficult, despite the fact that the woods were a fraction of the size they had once been when Agnes had lived and died within them. The mud was thick and sloppy underfoot, and we slid across the surface of it like we were trying to navigate a frozen lake. Somehow, we stayed upright, using each other for support and the tree trunks for leverage. When we broke through the endless sea of needles and branches onto the path, we were met by the sight of Hayley leaning against Agnes' tree, trying to catch her breath. Her eyes fell on us and she smiled through the tears coursing down her cheeks.

"I was so worried..." she started, wiping at her face with her sleeve. She gathered the pieces of herself quickly; deep breath, straight back, shrug of the shoulders. I pulled her into a bone crushing hug, regardless.

"We don't have time. The tree!"

Becca reached for the gas bottle in my hand but I yanked it back with a shake of my head. If this didn't work, and all we achieved was pissing Agnes off further, then I would bear the consequences – not Hayley, and not my sister. Though the identical looks in their eyes told me they understood my intentions, Becca was far too stubborn to agree to them. She swiped at the bottle with renewed energy. I evaded her fingers just barely and

Hayley stepped forward to wrap her arm around Becca's shoulders.

"Stay away. I'm going to torch this thing. If it doesn't work, you run and you don't look back."

Speaking with a strength I hadn't long possessed, I twisted the cap off the bottle and tossed it aside. As stupid as it might sound, I'd expected some kind of reaction from the yew tree when I emptied the contents of the can over it – dousing branches, trunk, and exposed roots as liberally as I could manage. It was a welcome relief when nothing did happen, beyond a few outraged insects scuttling from the crevices they had been hiding inside. I realised that I'd also expected more of an odour from the gas; maybe a stench not unlike the petrol station forecourt on a summer day, when the balmy air heats the gas as it spills out of the pump. Maybe it was the cold numbing my nose and dulling my sense of smell. It was a trivial enough concern that I didn't bother with it for more than a second. I turned to Hayley and Becca, hand extended for the book of matches that my sister had wedged in her pocket. She tossed them over with a grudging sort of compliance and Hayley leaned in closer to her to offer comfort. They both watched me with worried eyes.

I was all thumbs trying to strike the first match, and the second. The third one sparked against the side of the box at the same time that Agnes' battle cry carved through the trees. There was a crash and a crunch and a crack, all of which spanned the space of a moment, which was all it took for Agnes to tear down anything that stood in her path: she had made it to the woods, finally, and she was gaining ground.

I tossed the match before it could burn my fingers. It touched the base of the tree and smouldered, producing wisps of smoke that were promising. It sputtered out. A cry died in my throat and I lit another match in a fluid move. The building tension pressed against my chest and skull with such enormous weight that I thought both would cave in. I dropped the light, praying for a spark. Nothing caught.

"The gas isn't lighting!" The fear in my own voice was palpable. Gripped in my unsteady hand, the matches rattled inside their box.

"Is the tree too wet? Try again!"

"I am trying!"

"Try harder!"

"Why don't you try?!"

"I will!"

"It won't do much good." Hayley's voice was hollow – injected with none of the strain that ours were wrought with. It brought a swift end to our back and forth. Becca went quiet, as did I, so that the only sound remaining in the entire woods was that of Aggie ploughing through the brush.

"What?" It should have been a demand, however, I could hardly muster a timid peep. Frigid wind blew across the back of my neck. Goosebumps budded on my flesh.

"It won't do much good. It's not gas. Can't you tell by the smell?"

Hayley was more jovial, all of a sudden. Alarm bells clanged in my head, alongside those that continued to peel over at the postal centre.

"What..."

Becca didn't manage more than a word before Hayley cut through her with a laugh. A tree toppled nearby, heralding the monster. In response, a tear leaked from my eye before I could sink my teeth into my tongue to stop it.

"It's only water, Becca. Sometimes, you're so slow that I'm embarrassed for you."

I didn't want to confront the truth, though I had no choice, what with it staring daggers at me across the woods. I could feel Hayley's stare in a way I never had before. Cruel. Calculating. Scornful. Stealing myself with a breath, I turned to meet her head on. I let the matches fall from my hand.

"About time you caught on."

There was a smug grin cracking Hayley's pretty face in half, and my fingers twitched with the desire to beat it back into oblivion.

"Olly, what is she...?" Becca began, confused, as she peered between us.

Unwilling to offer a response, Hayley rolled her eyes. Before I could step forward to act as a buffer between the two, Hayley dove for Becca, swinging; not just fists, though, but the thick branch she had managed to conceal behind her back. Becca never saw it coming.

The branch struck the back of my sister's skull and she crumpled, totally boneless. The thud of contact was louder to my ears than Agnes, who continued to snarl as she circled the copse of trees amongst which we stood. Though I knew she was there, the witch made no move to advance, instead waiting on permission from the one who had been jerking her strings all along.

"I thought she'd never shut up," Hayley said. She stepped over Becca like she was a pile of discarded trash, and I knew that I had failed. I couldn't protect my little sister any more than I could protect myself.

"What are you doing?"

I didn't realise I'd been retreating until my back hit something solid. The tree. Its leaves tangled in my hair, berries gently thumping the crown of my head. I was sure it was mocking me. Hayley smiled again. The gesture was growing more sinister by the second. With her face bathed in moonlight, she was ethereal; no less beautiful for how unhinged she looked. Her gaze raked over me, lazily, as if she had already determined that I couldn't pose a threat to her, or jeopardise her endgame. It was difficult to admit to myself that she was probably right.

"I'm tying up loose ends, Olly." Her hands landed on her hips. "So... how about a little girl talk?"

9

DAY 12 – 20:33 HRS

"The tree! The tree must be the answer!" Mocking, Hayley pressed the back of one hand to her forehead. A smirk twitched at her lips, ruining her dramatic tableau.

She ducked her head as her shoulders shook with laughter. Body tense, I stared, not daring to move. Whatever this insanity was, it was new and untested. I couldn't be certain of how Hayley would react to anything, so I did nothing at all to avoid the risk of provoking her.

She continued, between chuckles, "You guys have watched too many shitty horror movies. Fire isn't like the supernatural cure-all, you know?"

I didn't. I'd obviously fallen for her manipulation, hook, line and sinker.

"Hollywood needs to use a little imagination, is all I'm saying. It's lazy writing. *'Set fire to the cursed book. Set fire to the possessed doll. Set fire to the haunted house.'* Does nobody think about the carbon monoxide emissions? There's a hole in the ozone layer, for God-sakes."

"Yeah," I said, managing to excavate my voice from somewhere deep within the narrowed passage of my throat. "Pollution is the real evil here."

I expected a more volatile reaction to my sarcasm but Hayley surprised me again with more laughter. When it petered out, leaving the imprint of a smile upon her face, I should have realised how far gone she was.

"You don't get it, do you, Olivia?" She purred my name, reminding me of housecat waiting for its hard-earned saucer of milk. "Real evil doesn't burn."

On cue, Agnes screeched, unleashing her fury at the moon. A shudder rippled through my body, starting at the base of my spine and finishing with my shoulders. Hayley watched me with a gaze that was somehow more predatory, more intimidating, than any I'd received from Aggie.

"What about *LostBoy*?" My tone was accusatory. Wounded. I'd wholeheartedly believed that *LostBoy666* had been the one wreaking havoc on Mildenhall, destroying our lives, and the realisation that I had been wrong all along stung badly. Hayley brushed me off like a piece of lint on her shoulder.

"The guy's a dick but he's not a murderous dick. Probably. Most he's guilty of is trying to get into my sister's panties."

"You let me believe..." I raged, only to be interrupted.

"Hey, you were the one that came up with that theory. I just went with it. It was pretty convenient, to be honest."

"I was worried about you. I cared about you!"

"You were worried about Charlie, Tiff, and Becca. You never gave a shit about me or Rose."

I shook my head in denial, unwilling to accept the accusation levied at me when I knew it wasn't true: I had been willing to risk my life for all of my friends, even Rose, who rubbed me the wrong way most days. As annoying and sour as she could be, I hadn't wanted to lose her - especially not to the kind of evil that roamed the woods of Mildenhall.

"You killed them all. You killed Mrs. Pedlow and Jennifer, too." I choked on my conclusion. "You killed your own sister."

Too busy picking dirt out of her nails, Hayley shot me a fleeting look.

"Actually, Agnes did all the leg work. I summoned her, but something round here had to change. I'm just sorry I lost my cat in the process."

The image of Magic – covered in blood and stuffed into the wall cavity – surged into my mind. Back at the museum, the guide Becca and I had spoken to had mentioned a sacrifice was required to wake the witch; this was the price Magic had paid for Hayley's ambition. Stowing his body inside Charlie's wall had helped sell the story of a troubled girl consumed by tales of witchcraft and curses.

"Your sister!" I spluttered, outraged. Hayley shrugged.

"Charlie was toxic. I did my family, and the world, a huge favour."

"How can you say that? That's sick!"

With a growl, Hayley stalked towards me and I struggled to hold my ground whilst my brain demanded I retreat from the threat. She was dangerous, unpredictable, and advancing on me with intent. However, she stopped a few feet shy of the yew tree, her features scrunched.

"Charlie was a waste of oxygen. I'm glad she's gone."

My mouth dropped open and I shook my head as disgust overwhelmed me. I had believed that Charlie and Hayley were close. As far as I'd known, they had shared everything with each other; clothes, make-up, secrets. Hayley had seemed so devastated when Charlie had vanished. All along she had been duping us with an *Oscar*-worthy performance.

"Were you jealous of her? Is that it?"

Hayley scoffed at the inference. "Now you sound like the crazy one. What exactly was I supposed to be jealous of? Drinking? Smoking? Failing all her classes? Oh, wait, maybe I was super envious of her creepy, internet boyfriend!"

She stuck her finger down her throat, miming a gag.

"If you weren't so self-involved, Olivia, then maybe you'd have noticed what was going on with Charlie. The drugs, the partying, the weekend hook-ups with that emo freak. My sister was a train wreck waiting to happen, and you were so wrapped up in yourself that you didn't have the slightest idea."

"That's not true..." I whispered, horrified and sick to the stomach with regret. "We talked all the time. Charlie would have told me..."

"But she didn't," snapped Hayley. Twigs and leaves crackled beneath her boot, and Agnes' head whipped towards the sound. The monster hung back, having clambered half way up a tall oak, where she perched to await her orders.

"She didn't talk to you. I bet she didn't even tell you about the fights she was having with our parents. Did you know they wanted us to go to family therapy? All because of *her*. I didn't deserve to be punished, I didn't do anything wrong; I'm the good daughter! Charlie was poisoning my family."

I couldn't help the giggle that burbled out of my mouth at the absurdity I was hearing. Hayley looked affronted but didn't make a move to wave over her monster.

"The good daughter? Do you hear yourself? You've killed five people!"

"Six," Hayley corrected, not at all phased by the escalating body count. Her tone was matter-of-fact as she added, "Why do you think Coach Rhodes was out from school today?"

"Coach?" I repeated, dumbfounded. "What did she do?"

"She chose Jennifer instead of me. Captain was supposed to be mine! I busted my ass all summer practicing. I guess I win by default now."

I couldn't seem to close my gaping mouth. The more Hayley

revealed to me, the less sense any of it made. How could something as inane as cheerleading motivate her to take a life?

"And what about the others, huh?" I grit out through my clenched teeth. My jaw cracked with the force I exerted, sending a ripple of pain into my ear. "Mrs. Pedlow? Rose? Tiff?"

"Hated piano lessons; on my last nerve; collateral damage." She ticked each corresponding explanation off on her fingers, listing them with a level of nonchalance I'd expect her to recite a grocery list with.

"You are insane."

"It's a spectrum. We're all on it somewhere."

My mind reeled, not up to the effort required to process Hayley's logic. The worst thing was, it all seemed to make perfect sense to her. She had cut six lives short – seven, if Magic counted – and was preparing to add one more to her ledger, yet there wasn't the smallest spark of guilt in her shrivelled heart.

"What about me? Where do I fit into your grand plan?"

Fury made my voice rough. Hayley quirked a brow at the audacity of me, given my precarious situation, but what was the point in trying to keep in her good graces?

"Honestly, it's nothing personal. I actually kind of like you. Well, you piss me off less than the others did, anyway. The free ice cream was great whilst it lasted." Her consolatory tone didn't blunt the sharp edges of the truth. I had been used, and she wasn't done with me yet. "It's just that I'm going to need a scapegoat for Becca, and you fit the bill."

I hadn't chanced a glance at my sister, needing to keep an eye on both Hayley and Agnes, but I did then. I took in her sprawled form, twigs tangled in her hair and her bandaged hand outstretched, like she was reaching out to me for help. She hadn't roused from the blow Hayley had delivered and I was starting to worry that maybe she never would. You heard about it all the time; a knock to the head, then lights out forever. I could feel my bottom lip wobbling, although I could do nothing to stop it.

"I'll tell them. I'll tell everyone what you did."

"Please do. It'll really help me sell my *'Olivia's gone crazy'* narrative."

One step closer. Two steps. Three. I held my ground with nowhere else to go.

"Seven people don't disappear without a trace."

"I told you, there'll be plenty of Becca left. Aggie only needs her soul. She's got no use for the rest of her."

High-pitched chattering – like a colony of bats flying overhead – pulled my attention back to Agnes. Taking my eyes off her had been a mistake as she was already at the base of her tree, crawling towards my sister on her wrecked limbs.

"Now, as much as I'd like to stand here all night and chat, I have homework. Plus I'm going to need an alibi for all of," Hayley circled her hand in the air, incorporating the four of us, locked in our deadly standoff, "this."

"You're not going to get away with it," I growled, temporarily willing to overlook how cliché the threat sounded. Hayley didn't bother to react, instead shoving her hands into her pockets and meandering back to the path. Over her shoulder, she called out to me, completely care-free.

"It's you that won't get away with it, Olly."

Hayley had been safe all along – never marked by the witch, as she wanted us to believe – and so, when Agnes dove over her head, she was in no more danger than she might have been from a kitten. In theory, neither was I. The thing was, I wasn't about to offer my sister up as the final sacrifice.

Agnes landed near Becca's head and stooped to roar right into her ear. My sister didn't stir and I had to shelve that concern in favour of procuring some sort of weapon to fend the creature off with. I hit the ground on my knees to scrabble around for a hefty branch, like the one Hayley had assaulted Becca with. Blindly, I searched through the leaves and soil, whilst I watched the monster's saliva drip into Becca's hair.

"Don't be stupid, Olly," warned Hayley from her position on the path. Apparently, she intended to watch, too - probably to ensure that the last stage of her plan went off without a hitch. I wasn't about to make that easy for her.

My hands curled around a thick, broken-off branch with moments to spare, and I raised it like a baseball bat to take a swing at Agnes, who hovered over my sister, jaw slowly unhinging. I yelled as I took the shot, feeling the force ripple through my arm and shoulder muscles when the branch made contact with the witch's head. It side-swiped her, knocking her down onto her back. The groan that rose on the night air belonged to Hayley, though.

"You're deluded if you think you can stop her."

"I don't," I muttered, narrowed eyes on the creature as it dragged itself back up to stand. "I just have to hold her off a little while."

Displeased, Agnes screeched at me as she shook off the fall like a dog shakes off rain water. She didn't turn on me, though, her piercing eyes instead swinging back to Becca. It was obvious that it was going to be more difficult than I'd assumed to distract the bitch.

"Becca, wake up!" I shouted at the top of my voice, readying my bat as Agnes crouched. "Becca! Come on! I need you..."

Crossing her arms, Hayley tutted, as if she considered me somehow overly dramatic. Hip popped, head cocked, nose wrinkled, she looked every bit the mean, disdainful cheerleader from all the teen movies I'd ever seen. For a second, I considered swinging the branch at her as opposed to Aggie. I shook myself free from those thoughts, drawing a few wide arcs with the limb and forcing the beast to hop backwards or risk being clipped. Attacking Hayley wouldn't serve any purpose when Agnes already had her orders, no matter how much my former friend might have deserved a beat down.

"Becca, get up!"

Drawing level with my sister, I jabbed the end of the makeshift weapon forward in the air like a spear. It missed the intended mark by inches but its presence in my hands at least seemed to deter Aggie from launching forwards. She ogled the sharp end with an almost wary eye, making me wonder how much humanity remained within her, and whether or not she could recall what the villagers had done to her all those years ago. If I'd have thought that appealing to her might have worked then I'd have dropped to my knees and begged for my sister's life, but I doubted it could be that simple. Instead I would keep pushing her back into the trees, where it would be harder for her to leap or clamber, and hope that would give us the opportunity to run.

At my feet, Becca moaned. It took all my self-discipline not to look down at her and to keep my gaze firmly locked on Agnes.

"What..." she slurred, hand clutching the back of her head as she raised herself from the ground. I didn't need to be looking at her to tell the exact moment she clocked Agnes; her startled mewl was the perfect indicator. Hysterical sobs soon followed, until the woods were alive with a combination of my sister's jerking breaths and desperate pleas.

"God, no... I don't want to die. *Please*, Agnes... Olly, I'm not ready. I can't..."

"You're not going to die!"

I didn't mean for it to resemble a snarl but it did, and I didn't have the time to fret over Becca's wounded feelings. The branch-spear was having less and less effect on Agnes, who was becoming more daring with how far and fast she chose to lunge at me. At one point, the glorified stick scraped her cheek, slicing a track in the pale and waxy skin that pulsed the same strange blood. Moonlight glinted off rows of snapping teeth, making them seem impossibly long and reminding me of how lethal Agnes was.

"When you get the chance, you run."

"Not without you. I'm not leaving you."

"I said get out of here, Becca!"

"Shut up! I won't leave you."

"God, this is so touching, but totally pointless. Let me spell it out for you: you run, you still die. Just give up, Olly, and at least you'll make it out of this in one piece. Being an only child isn't so bad."

Hayley's interruption simultaneously stunned Becca into silence and set fire to my blood. So much fury – scorching and intense – licked through my veins, searing my muscles. I chanced a glance at my sister, who was at the edge of my peripheral vision, bouncing on the balls of her feet as she prepared to act when the chance presented itself. There was no escaping this kind of fate, I knew, but I was going to keep swinging until the last second. If I got lucky, maybe I could take Hayley down with us.

"It has to be seven souls. Nothing else will work," said Hayley. "Nothing else can stop her."

Smug satisfaction oozed from her pores to saturate her voice. I longed to launch the branch at her as if it were a javelin. My anger swelled to immeasurable proportions.

"Do you ever get sick of hearing yourself talk?"

I rounded on Hayley before I knew what I was doing. I took my eye off the ball for hardly a second, and that was all she needed. Realising my mistake, I whipped back around to face Aggie. Using my distraction to her advantage, she had bolted straight for Becca. Her last target. My sister stilled, mouth open in a silent scream and hands raised to shield her face from the oncoming attack.

There was nothing I could do to help her. I had messed up. Now, Becca would pay with her life.

10

DAY 12 – 20:43 HRS

I didn't remember much about the day Becca was born. I was far too young to absorb much of it. There was a handful of memories, yellowed and fading at the edges, that I shuffled through on occasion: holding Dad's hand as we walked a narrow corridor with storks painted on the walls; handing Mom a posy of daisies I'd picked from the garden outside the hospital; and, lastly, being hoisted up to gaze at my brand new sister, sprawled out in a plastic crib.

I couldn't recall what I'd thought of her in that instant, when she'd been so new and novel to me. Maybe I'd been jealous, worried over this tiny usurper who'd come to steal my parents from under my nose. Maybe I'd been happy to have a playmate, especially one who resembled the baby dolls that were all over the commercials when I watched TV. Maybe I'd been indifferent – too small and naive myself to understand how this new life would forever alter the dynamics of everything I'd grown used to. Honestly, it wasn't too important how I'd felt in the beginning; no matter when the love had come, at some point in time, it had surged like an unstoppable tide to fill every crevice of space inside my body and mind until I was made buoyant by it.

Mothers describe it as 'the rush of love' that overwhelms them when skin first touches skin, eyes first meet eyes, and the pain of birth has ebbed. For siblings, there is no similar moment to catalogue, no universally recognised description that categorises what we have, and no expectation nor measure of the depth of what we will share. There is only us: soul mates, together, against the world.

That night, as we stood in Mum's Woods, with the gale buffeting our backs and the trees looming over our shoulders, that sentiment had never been more real.

I shrieked my sister's name as I wheeled to find Agnes ploughing into her. Two bodies slammed to the floor, rolling in a tangle of limbs, before skidding to a stop a few feet away. Somehow, Becca managed to land on top, her legs astride Aggie's thick waist and her knees dug into the dirt. Enraged, the witch bucked in an attempt to dislodge her but Becca managed to hold fast against the odds. The bandage had worked completely free of her hand, held in place tenuously by a single strip of tape. Thinking quickly, Becca grabbed both ends of the cloth and managed to gag Aggie with the length of it when her jaws drew perilously close. The thin material was torn to ribbons by Agnes' teeth inside a heartbeat.

"I got this!" squealed Becca, grappling with her attacker. "I'll keep her busy..."

The sentence hung unfinished in the air. Regardless, I knew exactly what Becca had been trying to convey: *I'll keep her busy, you work out how to stop her*. Problem was, all of our sources agreed there was no way to stop Aggie once she had gotten started. No way except the one I wasn't prepared to consider, because that would mean giving up my sister and allowing Hayley to win.

Hayley, who had caused all of this, and who had shown absolutely no remorse for the crimes she had committed under the guise of measuring out justice. *Hayley*, who had used the pain and suffering of a dead girl to yield more of the same. *Hayley*, whose warning knelled in my mind, loud and obnoxiously clear: *it has to be seven souls, nothing else will work.*

Hayley.

I don't know where I summoned the roar from – maybe the pit of my belly, maybe the depths of my soul – but I unleashed it, full of rage and wrath, as I tackled Hayley to the floor. She didn't expect it in the slightest.

She toppled, her back hitting a log with a crack that satisfied my need for retribution. All the air whooshed from her lungs – a noisy affair of raspy grunts – leaving her unable to do anything other than stare at me in a daze. I hadn't let go of the branch, so I raised it to shoulder height with clear intent. Hayley's eyes went wide but she couldn't pull in enough air to protest. Something akin to insanity slithered through my body, like a serpent, coiling around my brain to squeeze out the dregs of reason.

"I told you that you wouldn't get away with this."

My voice was a wretched creature, as ugly as Aggie and over which I had just as little control. Hayley appeared to recognise this, judging by the uneasy pull of her mouth and the way her breathing stuttered even when she recovered it.

"You won't hurt me. You're not like that." It pleased me to detect a note of uncertainty. Behind us, the sounds of Agnes and my sister wrestling, grappling for the upper hand, were all the encouragement I needed. It was them or us. I chose us.

"I think tonight has proved that we don't know each other very well at all."

With a cry escaping through gritted teeth, I drove the branch down in an arc that would be stunted by the right side of Hayley's head. As it happened, she had her own resolutions about giving in without a fight, and the kick she aimed at my ankles succeeded in taking me out. I managed to keep hold of my weapon as I landed on my side but that was where my luck gave, because Hayley scrambled over to me faster than I could evade her. She grabbed two fistfuls of my hair and yanked so hard in opposite directions that my yell couldn't cover the sound of hair breaking and roots being ripped from my scalp. I dropped the stick to clutch my head, hoping to negate some of the damage she was causing. Despite my attempts, Hayley came away with handfuls of my curls and I had to watch through the tears that had sprung to my eyes as she tossed them above her own head, laughing maniacally.

Lunging, I planted both palms in the centre of her stomach and pushed with all my might. She rocked back enough to allow me to crawl away on my knees, back towards the twisted tree, although Hayley was following to tug at my sneakers before I'd covered much ground.

"Get off me!" Through chance, I clipped Hayley's jaw with the toe of my shoe.

"Stop making this harder than it has to be!" she countered, diving right after me on her belly through the undergrowth. We wriggled along like that for a while – sliding up each other's bodies, grasping and gripping, shoving and tugging, in an effort to be the one who came out on top.

My goal was in sight: the base of the 'twisted tree' was dead ahead, at eye level, and I wasn't going to let anything stop me from reaching it.

"Come on, Olly, just quit it!" whined Hayley. She managed to seize my ankles and leaned down on them with her full weight to prevent me from inching away. In retaliation, I swiped a clod of dirt and small stones in my fist then flung them over my shoulder. Hayley swung her head out of the way, narrowly avoiding the cloud of grit and soil. From there, there was only one other option available to me, and I was no longer afraid to use it. Twisting my upper body backwards, I reached out to ram my index finger straight through Hayley's eyeball.

I felt the pop and the subsequent ooze of warm, wet fluid sliding over the tip of my finger. Any other moment of any other day, I would not have been capable of this: I would have been horrified. Right then and there, I was filled only with satisfaction, and slight disgust at the viscous liquid that was collecting under my fingernail.

"My eye! My eye! What have you done?!"

Hayley dropped back on her haunches immediately, hands flying up to cover her wounded eye. Blood streamed down her cheek, through her fingers, reminding me of the night that Becca had been impaled by the tree. Those thoughts spurred me on - the injustice of what Hayley had done to my sister, my friends, and our community, making me increasingly more vengeful.

She didn't try to come after me, she just sat there, howling and shaking whilst shock took hold of her. *Good*, I thought, *let her die scared, like the others did.*

I spared a glance for my sister – long enough to reassure myself that she was still alive. Still fighting. Aggie was scuttling backwards, dodging and weaving as Becca – now on her feet – threatened her with the tip of the branch I'd discarded.

Hold on, I thought, telegraphing it with every ounce of my will. *Just a few seconds longer, hold on.*

Stumbling to my feet, I threw myself at the 'twisted tree' and hugged the trunk with both arms as if it was my saviour.

My forehead slammed against the bark. The abrupt agony whited out my vision as well as conjured a sharp buzzing in my ears. Hayley's arms wound around my waist, pinning me, and I made no attempts to resist because the force of the blow had me reeling. I had to give her credit for the element of surprise. I'd thought she was down and dealt with, but I'd misjudged her again.

"I told you, burning this stupid tree won't do anything," Hayley jeered, right in to the shell of my persistently ringing ear. "Aggie is going to win... *I* am going to win... and your sister is gonna rot in Hell."

I could feel her shuddering against me, either as a consequence of her own wound or with the strength of her conviction. I sagged, half limp in her arms, the urge to give in, give up, and accept the inevitable, becoming overpowering. Hayley leaned closer so that her breath swished across my cheek and droplets of her blood pattered onto my neck. She seemed to want to say more but fighting through the pain had become impossible. My throbbing forehead gently kissed the trunk of Aggie's tree, my hands sliding round to caress it. I stilled, waiting for it all to be over, and Hayley loosened her grip on me. I realised, with a bitter smile, that I wasn't the only one who had misjudged their enemy.

"I... I wasn't trying to burn it..." I murmured, so low that Hayley had to press closer to hear me over the chaos behind us, "I was trying to use a little imagination."

I didn't see the smile drop from her features, or the remaining colour drain from her cheeks as she swallowed my words. I couldn't possibly have, from my position with my cheek against the tree, my right hand braced against the trunk, and my left hand buried in the tangle of branches, from which I'd seized a handful of yew berries.

Her grip was easy to break. It was easier still to spin around and smash the berries right into her open mouth. Before she could spit them out, I clamped her jaw closed with one hand and pinched her nose with the other. Like I was trying to force the family dog to swallow a pill. She fought to pull away from me, punching with both fists, kicking, and discovering that I wasn't such a pitiful adversary, after all. Hayley was strong and solid from years of cheerleading, but I had the advantages of height, weight, and righteous anger.

Tears, blood, and berry juice mingled on her chin. Hayley's remaining eye glared accusingly at me, the swollen lid having slid down to shutter the ruined one. Unable to hold her breath any longer, she had no choice but to swallow.

"Seven souls, bitch." My lip curled. "Save me a seat in Hell."

Fingers to my lips, I wolf-whistled as loudly as I could. The piercing intrusion stopped Agnes and Becca's battle dead – freezing both of them in a curious scene; Agnes hanging from a low branch by her hands and feet, whilst Becca pelted her with rocks she'd scrounged from the floor. At my side, Hayley shoved her fingers down her throat, desperately trying to trigger her gag reflex for real. I locked eyes with my sister, who was panting, panicked, and suddenly confused.

A beat. Silence from the surrounding woodland. Then, Agnes cocked her head, sensing a shift in something. Those malevolent eyes zeroed in on Hayley. A missile seeking a target.

She didn't have a chance to scream. Aggie was cantering towards her too fast for it to matter.

11

DAY 12 – 20:58 HRS

It was difficult to tell whose rage was louder - Agnes' or Hayley's. Either way, I didn't truly care. I threw myself aside at the sight of Agnes, airborne and close to taking me out. It would have been an accident, I knew. She only had eyes for Hayley, now. For the first time in hundreds of years - maybe her entire life - Agnes had been gifted agency over the choices laid out before her: kill the girl she had been ordered to, or savage the hand holding her leash. If I was in her shoes, I'd have found it an easy decision, too.

Grunting, I met the ground with my knees and palms. I flipped over onto my butt, torn between wanting to watch what was about to play out or listening to the flight response that had latently kicked in. I should have run, however, the desire to watch Hayley get what she deserved was too great to brush aside. I made up my own mind on the matter right as Agnes wrapped her arms around Hayley.

The screams never quit. They should have filled me with compassion or some sort of remorse for what I'd done, yet I floated above it all - completely detached. I registered Becca gripping my hand and I turned to her for a second. She looked like crap, for once – hair dishevelled, clothes ripped and muddied, and blood oozing from multiple wounds. She was alive, though. Something that our other friends were not.

I thought of them, then – Charlie, Rose, and Tiff. Whether it was that - my sudden yearning for their presence - or else their desire to watch as Hayley received her punishment that summoned them, I will probably never know.

They looked as they had in my vision. Too pale. Translucent. Gruesome. Despite it, I didn't shy away from them as they gathered at the base of the 'twisted tree' with their sights set on Agnes and her newest chew toy. Jennifer and Mrs. Pedlow joined them, the former wearing the shredded remnants of her cheerleading uniform and the latter with her neck crumpled concertina-style on one side. Coach Rhodes was the last to materialise. I was captivated instantly by the phantom whistle that dangled from her neck, swaying in front of a bite-mark that went all the way down to the bone.

"What's she going to do?" Becca tightened her hold on me until it was painful. The brief ache redirected my focus. I looked into her teary eyes and felt the moisture gathering in my own.

"She's going to finish what Hayley started."

With a sharp inhale, Becca shook her head, anguished. I pulled her into my side with one arm, allowing her the option of hiding her face in my collar if she found that she couldn't look. I, however, had no intention of turning away until it was done. Something inside me had hardened, and it remained to be seen whether that would turn out to be a good thing or not.

Hayley's garbled pleas faded into the rumble of the building wind and Agnes' cackles. Although a shudder ran through me, I kept an eye on Aggie and the other on the ghosts of the friends I had missed so much. Slowly, deliberately, and with an expression chiselled from stone, Charlie raised her arm to point her finger squarely at her sister. I held my breath as the others mirrored the action, animosity carved into their features. Even kind, placid Mrs. Pedlow suddenly seemed like a force to be reckoned with.

It was over faster than Hayley deserved.

Agnes leapt one branch then two higher, her prey fighting in her hold. When it seemed she was sure that we were all paying attention, she sank her fangs so enthusiastically into Hayley's neck that we heard the ripping of flesh from the ground. She drank ravenously for a few moments, Hayley's eyes rolling in her head and her mouth cavernous. No sound escaped her, which was both a blessing and a disappointment to my newly hardened heart.

The feeding didn't last long, and, as Agnes wrenched her jaws away, Hayley's neck snapped with the force. My gasp surprised me, but I was more stunned when Agnes seemed to intentionally meet my eyes. I found that I could read her like an open book: *this one's for us*, she seemed to say, without words – then, she dropped the body.

Hayley hit each limb on the way down. She landed on her back with a thud I'll hear forever in my nightmares. Every tiny muscle in her face was slack, and her good eye was fixed unseeing into the branches where Agnes hunkered, licking the blood from her lips.

I startled when Becca's hand touched my shoulder, drawing my attention away from Hayley.

"What now?"

I had no answers for her.

I wasn't left to ignorance for long, as it turned out. Starting at the roots of the 'twisted tree', the ground around us started to vibrate, as if rocked by an earthquake. Becca grasped my sleeve and I clung to her waist in return, both of us unsure of whether we should be running again or not. There was no way to tell if it was really over, as they say in the movies.

"Look!"

I followed the direction of Becca's finger, aimed at the spirits assembled around the tree. Rose was first to disappear in a puff of black smog that resembled an inkblot, with its tendrils stretched out in all directions. Tiff went the same way, offering me a morose smile beforehand. Together, Mrs. Pedlow, Coach Rhodes, and Jenny followed, without sparing a glance for those of us fortunate enough to have survived the ordeal. I didn't want to consider where they might be going: there was nothing I could do about that, after all. I comforted myself with the notion that, if Hayley went with them, they'd make sure there was no end to her suffering.

Soon, only Charlie was left. She stood beside her sister's corpse but refrained from looking at it. I couldn't tell if it was disgust or sadness that stayed her.

Letting go of Becca, I took hesitant steps towards Charlie. Our eyes locked. I opened my mouth - searching for the right words to construct my apology - then closed it again when I failed to find them. How exactly did you say you were sorry for ignoring your best friend's problems until they had killed her? Everything would sound trite; pathetic; insincere. Some wrongs are beyond the bounds of forgiveness.

Instead, I settled on the one thing I had felt in my heart since the moment I had realised that my friend was gone.

"I miss you, Charlie. I think I always will."

She didn't look away, just held me in her steady regard whilst the earth underfoot rolled and shook. Hayley's body bounced along with it, beyond repair and lifeless. I waited for some kind of sign: a smile, a nod, an incline of the head, but was crestfallen when I received none.

"Thank you for trying to warn me," I said, quieter, and Charlie acknowledged that at least with a deep shrug of her shoulders. "I wish I'd been a better friend, like you deserved."

She was already fading. Wisps of smog rolled off her body, taking pieces of her solid form with them. I continued to watch until the end, when the last shards of Charlotte Hill disappeared into the ether, leaving the world with her memory alone to remember her by. This much was clear to me from the final look in her eyes and the stern set of her features; I had not been forgiven. Maybe one day, I dared to hope. Eternity seemed like a long time to hold a grudge.

"Olly, get back!"

Frantic yells encouraged me away from the tree, just in time. The fire caught from the roots - sparking from nothing – to proceed along the trunk with ferocious hunger. The bark crackled, reminding me of cosy evening campfires and summer vacations with my friends that I had thought would last forever. These flames, though, were tinged blue at the tips, and that much I couldn't explain.

As the inferno swept higher, engulfing leaves and foliage with ardour, I raised my gaze to the topmost branch to see what had become of Aggie. Like the others, she was scattering to the wind in curling tentacles of vapour, so fast that the fanning flames had no chance to reach her. There was no happy ending here, for any of us. All that seven souls had bought Agnes Tippet was eternal damnation.

"I guess the witch got what she wanted." Appearing directly behind me, Becca seemed to pluck the thoughts straight from my mind.

"Not the witch," I said, softly. "This was all the Devil."

We shuffled away from the blaze when the heat from it began to warm our faces. Shortly, there would be nothing left of the 'twisted tree'. Given enough time, people would forget about the story of Agnes Tippet altogether, and children would no longer sing her rhyme in the schoolyard to frighten their playmates. I wished it could have been different and that Agnes could have found her peace, but the dice rarely land where we want them to.

The pop of a spark separating drew us to Hayley's body, lying within an arm's length of the tree. A spot on the shoulder of her jacket started to smoulder first, before the widening burn mark burgeoned into a crop of flames.

"She was wrong." My voice was tiny, like I was whispering into a black hole. The ground ceased its powerful rolling and I sighed my relief into the warming air.

"Who? About what?" Becca asked, creeping closer to me to lay her head on my shoulder. Some of her wounds were weeping and I knew we would have to take care of them before we tried to sneak back home. Nature would take care of everything else for us.

"Hayley," I replied, cocking my head at the girl at our feet. I wasn't a bit upset when the skin on her hand reddened, then blistered. That hand had wrought so much damage.

"Huh?"

I continued to gaze at Hayley, watching her once-perfect face darken and char - hiding all evidence of what Agnes had done to her.

"True evil does burn."

A thin smirk possessed my lips; a direct contrast to the tears that started to gush from my eyes with such force that it was like I'd turned the faucets on full blast.

The stench of singing flesh and burning hair was rancid, and would become too much to handle before I could see this thing out. It didn't matter, though. I didn't need to watch, because I was suddenly sure of one thing.

"True evil burns real well."

EPILOGUE

Half of Mum's Woods was lost that night before the station fire brigade managed to put out the blaze. A few days later, they cordoned off the rest of it permanently with sky-high chain link and barbed wire. There was no push back from the community.

The Hills buried what remained of Hayley the following week. Becca and I attended the funeral in head-to-toe black, our parents nearby to lend their support after such an unprecedented degree of loss. They scarcely let us out of their sights in those early days, and Dad had already begun to petition for a posting back to the USA before the smoke had cleared. He cited severe emotional trauma as his reason. Becca and I didn't fight him on it: we would both be glad to leave behind England and the ghosts of everyone she had taken from us.

The official story on Hayley was that she had been clowning around in the woods, trying to start a campfire, and wound up losing control of the situation. The story circulating school was slightly different: the student body, and many of the teachers, agreed that Hayley had been so distraught over her sister's disappearance that she hadn't wanted to go on a second longer without her. The fire, they claimed, had been far from accidental. It was hilarious how wrong that gossip could be.

The hardest part by far was the funeral. As I reached down to toss that clod of dirt onto the closed lid of the coffin, I had to bite my lip to stop myself from screaming out in temper. Hayley didn't deserve the pomp or ceremony that she had denied to others, and she didn't deserve anybody's grief. I got through it by pretending it was my moment to say goodbye to our other friends. Even Mrs. Pedlow, Coach Rhodes, and Jennifer crossed my mind, although my tears were for Charlie, Tiffany, and Rose.

Wherever we could, my sister and I didn't offer our thoughts on our friends, and most people respected those boundaries by not outright asking. They whispered plenty, though. Around school and the base, the adults referred to our group as 'troubled'. The other kids opted for the less tactful 'cuckoo for *Coco Puffs*'. Mom suggested therapy to us once but Becca's reaction was so extreme, so volatile, that it was never mentioned again. A change of scenery, we agreed, was all we needed to escape the funk we had slipped into. We had gotten in with a bad crowd but that was over - the danger had passed, and we had escaped unscathed. If only they knew.

The police never located the other bodies, though I didn't expect them to. If Agnes had hidden them then she had done it well, and - thinking back to the way she had sunk her teeth so eagerly into Hayley's neck - the other possibility doesn't bear considering. Not if we ever want to sleep again.

After that night, and the revelations it brought, Becca and I have grown so much closer that we almost inhale and exhale in sync. Trauma bonding, some people might call it. We opted to look on it as a strange blessing. Agnes' gift to us. An apology for what she had stolen. We shared a bedroom for three months, until we packed up that house in Mildenhall and boarded the plane home. Once we received the keys to our new house in

America, we both unloaded our boxes into the same bedroom without the need for discussion. It just felt right. That will change when college rolls around, but I've already vowed to come home every weekend and holiday that I can, and to call my sister every day. Where once those promises may have been empty, and designed to console the girl who was scared of being left behind, I mean every word of them now. I'd been prepared to die for Becca, and you don't let a love like that slip through your fingers because keg parties and Frat boys beckon.

That is, if I decide college is even for me. I'd been so certain of my future plan beforehand, but I no longer find the joy I once did in music and singing. In fact, I realised six months after the fact that I hadn't sung a note since the day before Charlie had disappeared. Maybe I never will. Or maybe, one day, sometime in the future, I'll catch myself humming along to the car radio, and everything will be as it should be. For me, at least.

Back in RAF Mildenhall, nothing will be the same. Not in another six months, not in six years, not in six decades. Whether the people there know it or not, evil roamed that land and claimed it for its own. That's not the kind of wound that heals with time, it's the kind that festers and necrotises: the kind that kills. If fire truly can't cleanse, then God help them all when those fences rust and fall down.

I guess I've rambled enough. With the pages I've filled, it sure feels like it to me. Who knows? If you didn't pass out from boredom or develop narcolepsy half way through this whole mess, then I could be destined to be a writer. I think I could live with that. Right now, though, I'm content to figure it out as I go along.

I've got the time.

Olivia,

Whilst this piece was most certainly a journey, I don't think that you've truly taken the assignment seriously, or made an effort to understand what is expected from a college admission essay. Although the directive *(Discuss an accomplishment, event, or realization that sparked a period of personal growth and a new understanding of yourself or others)* lends itself to your prose, in theory, a typical admission essay should be rooted in <u>FACT ALONE</u>. It should <u>not</u> read like a dollar store young adult novel!

I realise that you and your sister have had an incredibly difficult time prior to returning to America, but I can't help you in this period of adjustment if you refuse to cooperate. Should you wish to proceed with your applications, I'm more than happy to run through some more appropriate ideas with you. You certainly have a flair for writing, so I'm certain you can meet this challenge head on with the right guidance!

Please see me tomorrow during morning recess.

Miss. Franks (English Lit.)

AUTHOR'S NOTE
MUM'S WOODS – A BRIEF HISTORY

I first learned of the Mum's Woods witch completely by accident. Around twelve years ago, (when I was living at an RAF base in the south of England that was purported to be haunted), I stumbled across an online message board that contained this and a handful of other paranormal stories. Intrigued, I looked deeper into the tale. All I could find was a few articles that suggested a 17th century accused witch haunted the old woods behind USAF (RAF) Mildenhall. Whilst most details were scant, these articles agreed that the unfortunate and nameless woman had been staked to the ground using yew branches, then left to die.

For various reasons, the story stuck with me, only to resurface in my mind over a decade later when I was asked to write more books in the Base Fear series. The Mum's Woods witch felt like the perfect inclusion: part ghost story, part creature feature, and part historical recount of what life was like for many women (and men) in a time where king and country were gripped by witch hysteria.

Whilst the 'twisted tree', Agnes Tippett, and the details of her life are entirely of my own creation, the county of Suffolk did indeed play host to the famed and feared Witchfinder

General, Matthew Hopkins. In a campaign of terror that lasted only three years (1644-1647), Hopkins and his associates accused, tortured, and executed over 100 alleged witches. His brutal methods - including using sleep deprivation, the swimming test, and blunt knives to extract confessions – are outlined in his book, 'The Discovery of Witches'. When I visited Moyse's Hall (as featured in the story) to carry out my own research, I spoke with a historian who explained that there simply aren't enough surviving records to be certain of exactly how many innocents were put to death by Hopkins and his ilk. Some believe the number to be close to 500, whilst others estimate it to be double that.

In my search for the truth, I was unable to uncover concrete evidence as to whether an accused witch was put to death at Mildenhall or not. Many of the locals I spoke with knew of the woods, nestled behind the old postal centre on camp, yet had no idea as to who – or *what* – they were haunted by. The one thing they could agree upon was that Mum's Woods was an eerie place with an oppressive atmosphere, where grown airmen feared to tread after dark.

Perhaps one day, I will get the chance to investigate the woods for myself, which is no easy feat given that they are tucked away behind the station fence! Until then, though, I must close my eyes and imagine the muted whisper of the breeze caressing the branches of the yew trees, and the laughter of a forlorn girl who seeks salvation.

Printed in Great Britain
by Amazon